FALL, BOMB, FALL

FALL, BOMB, FALL

Gerrit Kouwenaar

TRANSLATED FROM THE DUTCH BY MICHELE HUTCHISON

PUSHKIN PRESS

Pushkin Press
Somerset House, Strand
London WC2R 1LA

Copyright © The Estate of Gerrit Kouwenaar, 1950, 2023
Original title *Val, bom*
Published by Em. Querido's Uitgeverij bv, Amsterdam
and Uitgeverij Cossee bv, Amsterdam
English translation © Michele Hutchison, 2025

First published by Pushkin Press in 2025

Published by arrangement with Cossee International Agency

ISBN 13: 978-1-80533-243-5

All rights reserved. No part of this publication may be reproduced, stored in a retrieval system or transmitted in any form or by any means, electronic, mechanical, photocopying, recording or otherwise, or for the purpose of training artificial intelligence technologies or systems without prior permission in writing from Pushkin Press

The publisher gratefully acknowledges the support
of the Dutch Foundation for Literature

**Nederlands letterenfonds
dutch foundation
for literature**

A CIP catalogue record for this title is available from the British Library

The authorised representative in the EEA is
eucomply OÜ, Pärnu mnt. 139b-14, 11317, Tallinn, Estonia,
hello@eucompliancepartner.com, +33757690241

Designed and typeset by Tetragon, London
Printed and bound in the United Kingdom by Clays Ltd, Elcograf S.p.A.

Pushkin Press is committed to a sustainable future for our business, our readers and our planet. This book is made from paper from forests that support responsible forestry

www.pushkinpress.com

1 3 5 7 9 8 6 4 2

FALL, BOMB, FALL

1

THE BOY STOOD at the sitting room window, staring outside. His jaws chewed away mechanically at an apple. The maid on the other side of the street had just finished cleaning the windows with a chammy leather and climbed the front steps, lugging a bucket and stepladder. Her skirt lifted in the process. He caught a good glimpse of her startled thighs before the door slammed shut behind her. The boy slowly resumed his chewing. It was around five in the afternoon and the streets were deserted. The spring light was a yellowish pink and the treeless road (of which he could see exactly twelve identical houses) seemed all the more like a theatre set because of it.

The boy stared at the closed door and tried to imagine how much fun it would be if he possessed a kind of magic spell with which he could control everything and everyone. As he tried to imagine this, he felt a great urge to close his eyes, but restrained himself and allowed only his head to fall against the glass with a gentle thud. Oh to be omnipotent! he thought. I could wish something and really focus my mind on it and then it would happen. The maths teacher suddenly collapsing at his desk, his wooden dividers clattering to the floor. Heart attack, the doctor would say, but I'd know better. I'd spot an attractive girl and make a wish: *cast yourself slavishly at my feet, adore me*, and she would immediately obey my unspoken command. But I'd do good deeds, too, with my amazing powers, he added hastily in his mind. Good deeds too. I would save the world from Hitler.

But the sudden intervention of conscience was accompanied by an overwhelming feeling of boredom. He threw the half-eaten apple into the bin and turned on the radio. 'Ode to Joy'. Everybody united in brotherhood. The Wishing Hat and the Bottomless Purse, he thought. Romanticism, he thought, schoolboy romanticism. A word from his vocabulary exercises – in the negative sense: excessively poeticising.

The boy chuckled to himself and listened to the music, wondering whether he actually liked it. No, he thought, but of course I'd tell everyone I thought it was wonderful. *It's very moving*, I'd say, resting my chin in my hands. I'd know I was lying but I'd maintain the pretence. There's a manual on adolescence in the bookcase, a guide for unimaginative parents. It explains what an adolescent is like; these are the symptoms, it says. But in terms of appearance: mainly spots. I don't have any spots and no one can check the rest, he thought with as much satisfaction as shame. He slowly turned around. His mother was sitting at the table doing her mending. She looked up and gestured silently at the teapot.

'Yes, please,' he said.

'Would you pour it yourself then,' she said.

'You too, Mum?' he asked. His mother nodded. As he carefully filled the teacups, he thought to himself: that's going well, she's stopped complaining when I say Mum instead of Mother.

'Shouldn't you be getting on with your homework?' his mother asked.

'I've barely any to do,' he replied. 'The holidays start tomorrow afternoon.'

'That's no reason to cut corners today,' she said. 'And you know Uncle Robert and Aunt Lise are coming to dinner, which always makes for a late night.'

Her son didn't respond. They drank their tea. The boy got up and went to stare at his mirror image in the glass doors of the bookcase. As he pretended to listen to the radio, he let his gaze slide along the spines. Stijn Streuvels' *War Diaries*: the German army advancing on Flanders, the hot August sun; German cavalry – *Ulans* bearing lances with flags on them; metal helmets shaped to protect the back of the neck. And: Barbusse's *Under Fire*. And Remarque's *The Road Back*.

Now there was a new war, but hardly any fighting. His history teacher had said it would come, though. The Netherlands surely would be unable to stay out of it this time. Sometimes the man had lengthy political discussions with a German girl, one of the Jewish immigrants in his class. A nice girl who wore one of those Tyrol waistcoats, a dirndl outfit like an Alpine peasant. Liselotte Stengel. Of course Germany would lose the war again. And a lot of people would die again. War is terrible, death is terrible, he thought. That run-over girl on the road. He was on his way home from school. An enormous crowd had gathered and the run-over girl, the headless girl, lay in the middle of the circle of silent, staring people. Her head was gone, there was just a pulpy red patch. You couldn't even see any hair. A lorry had driven smack-bang over her head, a lorry with double wheels. And the driver sat on the pavement crying and nobody would look at him. One man kept shouting, 'Make way everybody, make way. Does anyone have a sheet?' And another, 'Is there a doctor around?' Like that would be any use. But nobody looked at the driver. Everyone looked at the dead girl, lying flat on her back on the road. Her feet neatly aligned, high heels, a green sweater and very pointy breasts, and no head. Was she blond, dark-haired? Who knew. But dead, oh is that what death looks like? He saw it and went home and only days later did he feel sad. It gave him suffocating dreams like in that film, a jungle film, a man swallowed by a crocodile.

The slobbering jaws closed and only his hat was left floating. There was a dark patch on the surface of the swamp water. It was a film with an adult rating.

What if his father or mother were to die? Would I cry, he wondered. Would I mind if the war came here? He slowly shook his head. I'd love it, he thought. In fact, I want it to happen. I know it's repugnant to wish for war, but I'd love it. It would be exciting. Excessively poetic, he thought, worse still. Abhorrent, he said, almost audibly. He helplessly rubbed his hands together and felt his whole body becoming warm.

Maybe I don't wish for it, he thought then. Maybe I don't actually know what I wish for, what I actually want. I have thousands of thoughts. Maybe I'm abnormal. Imagine if we got bombed, imagine German planes appeared above the city this very instant. A bomb in this stupid, colourless street would be absolutely fantastic. Burning houses, twelve in a row! Imagine the whole street going up in flames, our house too, and we'd lose everything. We've already got air-raid shelters. And my history teacher says we won't stay out of it this time. We won't stay out of the shelters where all you can do now is urinate and have sex. Air-raid shelter: thirty-five people. Mass grave. Bombs in the middle of the night when you're asleep. Women running down the street half-naked. The desecration of corpses. A photograph from the Spanish Civil War came to mind, a hideous picture of a woman hung by fascists from a bell-rope in a church tower; flies swarming around a naked body with a shaved, bloodied scalp.

The boy shook his head and returned to the window before pressing his head to the glass again.

'Get on with your work, lad,' his mother said in a warm but insistent tone. He responded only with a grunt, thinking: she's right. My homework. I'm perverse, I'm a lech. I wish for appalling things. Does everyone have thoughts like this? Maybe my wishes will come true. Maybe I *am* omnipotent, only I don't know my own desires yet. They say we have souls. Imagine if it happened. And my homework, my homework. Yes, you're right, Mum. You're right. But I do so wish something would happen. I wish I dared say that I hate Beethoven. I wish Beethoven would be rudely interrupted – ladies and gentlemen listeners, a sad announcement. We are at war. Hoorah! Hoorah! Anyway, I never do my homework well enough. Your son could be one of our best pupils if only he applied himself more. He's rather playful. Yes, playful, he plays with bombs. Oh I wish – I wish a bomb would fall.

'Karel!' his mother cried.

The boy didn't make a sound. He stared at the lifeless street through the reflection of his own nose. A small child ran along the pavement rolling a metal hoop. May supreme powers inhabit me! I want that little boy to drop dead this instant. He inhaled deeply through his nose. He opened his eyes wide. I will strike him down with my death-stare, he thought. Fall down, die! I, Karel Ruis, say to you: die on the spot, little boy with your metal hoop. Fall, bomb, fall!

He allowed a quiet hum in the back of his throat to swell, right through Beethoven's final chorus. The little boy disappeared skipping into the cheesemonger's shop, The King of Cheese. The crown prince of cheese. Failed, he thought. He turned around and left the room, his head hanging.

2

Karel had installed himself at his desk in his bedroom. He opened his school diary. The motto of the day was: 'Today is what you make of it.' Yawning, he closed the diary and started to leaf through his history book. He paused on a photo for a while, captivated. 'Hitler in Vienna (1938)' was its caption. To the right a row of helmeted uniforms, one of whom was holding a raised banner. The dictator's right hand was raised to shoulder height. A few officers looked on warily. In the background there was a monumental building that looked quite a lot like the local municipal theatre.

Karel took a pack of cigarettes from the desk drawer. He opened the window and blew out little puffs of smoke. The bell rang in the hall. The boy leaned out of the window. Uncle Robert was standing on the doorstep: a round, protruding belly topped off by a grey hat. Uncle Robert was carrying his overcoat over his arm, he raised his hat and dabbed his wonderfully bald head with a folded white handkerchief. Then Uncle Robert shuffled inside. Karel went to his bedroom door and opened it a chink. He heard his mother welcoming Robert.

'Has Lise been held up?' she asked. His mother had a husky voice which always sounded slightly accusing. The other voice was jovial and chuckled a lot. Uncle Robert had a musical voice.

'Lise sends her apologies,' he replied. 'She'll be here in a minute. She's still shopping. Oof, it's warm for the time of year, Cora,' he said, puffing exaggeratedly.

'If you want to freshen up, feel free to use the bathroom. The green towel is for guests,' Karel's mother said. 'I must get back to the kitchen, but Philip will be home shortly.'

Karel heard Uncle Robert climbing the stairs and quickly shut his door, thinking: Cora and Philip, yes, that's what my parents are called. Nice names. Names that don't actually suit them at all. Mother never calls Father Philip and Father never calls Mother Cora. Getting married rendered them nameless. They passed their names on to their children. My brother is called Philip Lodewijk Robert and my sister Cora Alide, but I was the third child, so there wasn't much left for me. They'd exhausted their imagination. They just called me Karel, Karel and no second names, after some senile great uncle. If there'd been a fourth child, he probably wouldn't have been given a name at all. My mother always says, 'When I was a young girl I detested boys who were called Karel; boys called Karel were always louts. Louts they were,' my mother says. 'And now,' she says emphatically, 'my own son is called that. Barmy, isn't it?'

Yes, totally barmy. And she doesn't say anything else, no additional explanation, nothing in mitigation, no gentle ruffling of her youngest son's hair – nothing! She abandons her youngest son for him to fall prey to a great feeling of despair. 'Despair!' Karel repeated loudly. 'World, I'm an unwelcome third child,' he said, his nose in the air, 'and today is going to be what I make it. But tomorrow the holidays start. Tomorrow the government has decided for me.'

He heard the soft splashing of water in the bathroom. Uncle Robert is cooling his hairy wrists, he thought. And now he's rinsing his mouth. Now he's spitting the water out. He's drying his blubber-neck with the green guest towel and panting away. Uncle Robert is a very different man from my father. He doesn't wear woollen Jaeger underwear but pale blue Interlock. He wears red silk pyjamas and he powders and perfumes himself after shaving; he keeps his shaving kit in a leather pouch with a zip. Vanity case: special scissors for trimming hair from nostrils, nailfile, iodine ointment, cotton wool, skin cream, alum block. Uncle Robert is a very different man from my father. Uncle Robert is a proper dandy, my mother says. And when he gets hot, he says *oof* in a terribly old-fashioned way!

A knock on the door. Karel quickly opened a couple of books. It was Uncle Robert. The heavy man rubbed his hands together. The scent of eau de Cologne filled the small bedroom.

'Hello Karel, how are you my boy?' Uncle Robert cried, stepping toward him with an outstretched hand.

'Hello Uncle,' the boy said, shaking the clean fat hand.

'Working hard?' asked Uncle Robert.

'Yes, homework,' Karel explained, as though his uncle could mean any other kind of work.

'Wonderful, wonderful,' Uncle Robert said, chuckling. He continued to laugh with a deep, reverberating 'haha', his face cheerful. He had entered the room now, which made it seem even smaller.

'A snug little place to study,' Uncle Robert said, nodding vigorously. He sat down on the divan bed and cast a quick look around. He arranged himself very carefully, shoulders hunched as though he was in a tent.

'What kind of homework are you doing?' he asked.

'History,' said Karel.

'Ah, history,' replied Uncle Robert as he lay down on the divan bed and undid some of his waistcoat buttons. 'Have you already got to Le Roi Soleil?'

'We had him ages ago,' said Karel. 'We're in the middle of the French Revolution now.'

'Ooh,' said Uncle Robert, '*liberté, égalité, fraternité*. That's an important period, boy! Pay good attention to those lessons. It's the start of our culture. Our liberal society. An exciting era! *Les hommes naissent et demeurent libres!*' Uncle Robert cried. He got out a silver cigar case and intently fingered a dark-brown Havana. 'You don't smoke cigars, do you?' he asked.

'No, not yet,' said Karel. If only he'd leave, he thought.

'But I do have some cigarettes,' said Uncle Robert, 'ladies' cigarettes. Would you like a ladies' cigarette, Karel?'

'Yes please, Uncle,' the boy said, before slotting the slender stick loosely into the corner of his mouth. Uncle Robert clamped the cigar between his teeth as he patted the fat rolls of his neck with the flat of his hand.

'Well, well,' said Uncle Robert. 'Are you learning French too? Of course you're learning French,' he said, scratching his chest. 'Are you good at French? French is a very important language. In fact French is the most important language. Pay good attention during your French lessons, Karel!'

Uncle Robert squeezed his eyes half shut, saying, 'Tell me what *l'encre* means!'

'Ash,' said Karel.

'No,' said Uncle Robert, 'that's wrong. The first question I ask and you get it wrong. *L'encre* means ink. Ash is *la cendre. La cendre de ma cigarette,* see?'

'Yes, the ash of my cigarette,' said the boy.

'Good,' said Uncle Robert, staring at the ceiling. 'Let's continue our lesson. What does… *l'enfant* mean?'

'The child,' replied Karel.

'Correct,' said Uncle Robert, 'and *le sable?*'
'Sand,' said Karel.
'Excellent, excellent,' said Uncle Robert. 'And *la tuile?*'
'The roof,' said Karel.
'Wrong,' said Uncle Robert, 'a common mistake. Roofing tile. *Un toit en tuiles* is a tiled roof.'
'*Un toit en tuiles,*' repeated Karel.

Uncle Robert looked at his nephew as though he wanted to tell him something very important. His bottom lip sagged and his small nicotine-stained lower teeth came into view. He sighed deeply. 'Well then,' he said before getting up and brushing the ash from his waistcoat. 'You knuckle down to your work, boy. I'm off to keep your mother company for a while.' He gave Karel's upper arm a whack and left the room.

The boy stretched out on his warm bed and patted his neck with the flat of his hand. 'You knuckle down to your work, boy,' he muttered. He looked at the dark-blue wisps of smoke that floated uneasily through his room. It must be nice to have a man like that as a father. A man who instils awe in you without you being afraid of him or despising him. A man who gives you a cigarette when you are seventeen years old, and who wears pale-blue underwear. A modern gent. An enlightened spirit who lies down on your bed like a classmate.

Karel's mother didn't like Uncle Robert. Uncle Robert had had a son who'd died when he was about twenty. Uncle Robert had made the boy study so hard he'd come down with consumption, said Karel's mother. The boy had to work so hard it killed him.

'Karel!' his mother called out from the bottom of the stairs. I'll have to run to the shop, Karel guessed, but it won't kill me. Two ounces of luncheon meat, two ounces of bonbons, half a pound of assorted biscuits, a packet of cornflour. He unscrewed his fountain pen and walked to the kitchen holding it.

'I can't understand where they've all got to,' his mother said, harried. 'They were all supposed to be coming home early and still no sign of them. Half past five has come and gone and I'm stuck with that man. Go on, you keep the man company. I need to check on the food.'

'Alright,' said Karel, screwing the cap back on his fountain pen. He went into the sitting room. Uncle Robert was sitting in a deep armchair in front of the window. He was writing something and wearing a black pair of owlish spectacles. There was a jug of jenever in front of him. He merely nodded at Karel and carried on writing. Now and then he paused and took a sip, or poured himself a new glass. He suddenly looked worried. Karel felt a little self-conscious and quietly sat at the table, sneaking looks at his fat uncle over the evening newspaper. Once his uncle had refilled his glass three times, he put the written sheet of paper in an envelope, added the address and then stowed the envelope in his wallet. He took off his glasses and gave his nephew a thoughtful look.

'Well, boy,' he said. His face was dripping with sweat and suddenly appeared to be mapped with grey folds. 'Come a little closer,' said Uncle Robert, 'I want to discuss something with you in private.' He paused for a moment to drain his glass with a flick of the wrist, then he continued, practically at a whisper. 'You're old enough to keep a secret, aren't you?' Karel nodded. In the kitchen he could hear his mother humming a hymn. She hummed the hymn in an acerbic tone and behind him the radio issued white noise and no music. He gulped. 'Yes, Uncle,' he said.

'I know what you're thinking,' said Uncle Robert. 'You're thinking: is this really Uncle Robert, my jolly tub of an uncle? Perhaps you're thinking: he's had too much to drink.'

'No, Uncle,' said Karel.

'It doesn't matter. It doesn't matter what you think of me,' said Uncle Robert. 'As long as you understand that most people pretend to be different than they really are.'

'Yes, Uncle,' said Karel.

'Now then,' said Uncle Robert, 'you know what everybody knows about me – that fate has given me a serious battering. I could have been a concert pianist but a cricket ball broke four of my fingers and ended my career. I had a promising son, who died unexpectedly. I had a house which burned to the ground. I had a second house which also burned to the ground. I've got a third house, which will surely burn down too. Did you know all of that?'

'Yes, Uncle,' said Karel. 'You've told me often enough.'

'Correct,' said Uncle Robert, 'one cannot be informed early enough of fate's shenanigans. But have you ever asked yourself how I managed to remain such a cheerful person, despite all this misery?' He gave his nephew an almost triumphant look, but the boy didn't reply, he just sat there feebly, sunk deep in the old man's armchair.

'That's because,' Uncle Robert said, beginning to speak faster as he glanced at his watch, 'that's because I have a secret. There is a thing of joy in my life that gives me the strength to bravely weather fortune's blows. But now we are at war,' he said and his voice grew sad. 'We eat our bread and our meat, we drink our jenever, we smoke our cigars. But for how long? We're acting as though nothing has happened, and we wait. I wait and I'm still a fat jolly fellow, but my joy is in peril.'

'What is your joy?' Karel asked. I'm seventeen, he thought and I'm asking a man of fifty what his joy is. How dare I, he thought, proud and astonished.

At that moment the doorbell rang. As Karel heard his mother walking to the hall, Uncle Robert said, 'I will tell you later, not now. Listen,' he whispered agitatedly. He took the letter out of his wallet and pressed it into Karel's hand. 'I need you to deliver this for me on Saturday afternoon,' he said. 'A lady will receive you and she will give you a letter for me in reply. You must bring it to me. But don't mention it to anybody, not to your parents or to Aunt Lise.' Uncle Robert broke off. He quickly wiped his face with his freshly folded pocket handkerchief as though he were taking off a theatre mask. He made a few vigorous swings of the arm and patted his bulging waistcoat with his fists. 'Haha,' he chuckled, 'haha, good old Karel. Here, light another cigarette, boy.' His eyes were still vacant, but his face was filled with cheer again. In the hall, Karel's mother was talking to Uncle Robert's wife. Karel got up and turned the radio dial. Music, he thought, happy music.

Aunt Lise came in, accompanied by Karel's mother. Uncle Robert kissed his withered wife's hand.

'Is the lad smoking?' Mrs Ruis asked.

'Just this once, no harm in it,' Uncle Robert said.

Karel laid his burning cigarette in the ashtray. 'Hello, auntie,' he said.

'Hello dear boy,' the skinny little Indonesian woman said. Under her narrow shoulders, her heavy lace blouse furrowed shapelessly. She stood on tiptoes, grabbed Karel by the back of his neck and kissed him on both cheeks. Her lips were hard and rough, they skidded over his skin like sandpaper. When the boy went to pick up his cigarette again, he realised that his mother already had taken it, ashtray and all, to the kitchen.

A moment later, his father came home and then his brother and sister.

The sitting room was filled with grown-up voices. His

father and his brother were standing with Uncle Robert, a drink in their hands.

'Yes,' said Mr Ruis, 'all leave has been suspended, the situation is tense. But I expect it will all fizzle out again.'

They arranged themselves around the table. Mrs Ruis served up. They ate vermicelli soup from their best Sunday service without speaking. Uncle Robert ate with gusto. He'd tucked his napkin into his starched collar. When his plate was empty, he said, 'That soup was delicious, Cora. Would your maid be piqued if I gave her a little something?'

'I don't have a maid,' Karel's mother said. 'I haven't had a maid for a year. I do all the cooking myself.'

Karel's father ate with an absent smile on his face. His mother asked whether everyone had enough gravy. During dessert, Uncle Robert said to Mr Ruis, 'Young Karel has informed me that his school holidays start tomorrow. I've already told him that he might come and stay with us for a few days.'

'Very kind of you,' said Mr Ruis, 'as long as he doesn't neglect his schoolwork.'

'No, I'm sure he won't,' said Uncle Robert. 'We'll take a morning stroll in the woods,' he said. 'It's delightful at this time of year. And in the afternoon we'll take tea at the farmhouse café. And in the evening we can go to the pictures.'

After dinner, they had coffee in the conservatory. The men smoked cigars and the women had ladies' cigarettes. Karel didn't smoke and sat on a low chair. 'Karel already smoked before dinner,' his mother said.

The boy didn't listen to the conversation. In the newspaper he read about masked car bandits and how on a deserted heath a girl had been assaulted by a miscreant. He heard the downstairs neighbour's children playing with a ball in the garden. The geraniums in the window box were in bloom. Later on, a glass of liqueur was served with a small biscuit. At eight o'clock, Uncle Robert said it was time they were going.

'Fetch their coats, will you, Karel,' said his mother. Karel fetched Aunt Lise's coat, her fox stole and her hat with a veil, and Uncle Robert's overcoat and hard, grey hat. He entered the room buried under the pile, then helped his aunt into her coat.

'You're becoming a real gentleman,' she giggled coquettishly. 'Do you already have a girl, Karel?' she asked.

'No,' said Karel behind her back.

'Come, come,' said Cora Alide. 'Don't be so modest, little brother. He's got ten, aunty,' she said. 'He's a real Don Juan.'

'It's pronounced Don Hwan,' said Karel. 'You say a Spanish J like a Hw sound.' Am I imagining it, he thought in confusion, or is auntie deliberately pressing her bust against my hand? She kissed him again on both cheeks and now he didn't just feel the rasp of her dry lips but also the soft wet tip of her tongue.

'See you in a couple of days then, Karel,' she said.

Uncle Robert gave him a long, firm handshake. 'We have a deal then,' he said emphatically. 'I'll be counting on you, whatever happens.' Karel noticed that something had been left behind in his hand. A rolled-up piece of paper. He quickly slipped it into his pocket. As soon as he was back in his bedroom, he got it out: it was a ten-guilder note. He sat down delightedly at his desk and looked at the letter Uncle Robert had given to him.

'Mrs R. Mexocos,' he read. He had to chuckle. Uncle Robert is in love, he has a mistress. He's a real dandy, an old *bon viveur*. He's had enough of his saggy, jaundiced wife. He's taken a mistress with a foreign name.

He pulled out a few books and began to study with a sigh. He read, 'The dictator was not yet sufficiently feared or revered. He therefore had a law passed authorising the Revolutionary Tribunal to pass death sentences without witnesses or right of defence, on moral certainty of guilt alone.'

Karel really did shut his eyes now and heard the dividers clattering to the floor. The maths teacher sentenced, on moral conviction of guilt alone, he thought.

His thoughts sprang to Uncle Robert. Uncle Robert had said, 'There is a thing of joy in my life that gives me the strength to bravely weather fortune's blows. But now we are at war.' War? He smelled his hand. The blows of fate and the twinkling whites of Aunt Lise's eyes. He smelled his hand and rubbed the spot on his cheek where Aunt Lise's wet tongue had touched his skin.

3

THE PRESSURE of the metal headphones on his ears woke him up. His right ear was numb, as though it had been folded over for quite some time. He slid the painful headband from his head and laid it behind him, next to the crystal set, which he kept in a cigar box. He instinctively began rubbing his sore ears. He opened his eyes momentarily to check his luminescent alarm clock: it was past three. He closed them again immediately. He knew he wasn't yet fully awake and wanted to go back to sleep again as quickly as he could. I've only slept a couple of hours, he thought. He stretched out and rolled onto his side. It's soft, it's soft, he thought. The night and the half-sleep were a vast lukewarm bath in which he drifted motionless. The stately bars of the Dutch national anthem came into his mind. He remembered that he'd heard it just now on his headphones, a full orchestra, and it had faded out, and tick-tock, tick-tock. He hadn't heard the clock strike twelve, he must have fallen asleep to the ticking of the studio clock.

The sound of voices coming from his parents' bedroom, which was next to his, reached his ears. They sounded agitated but still reasonably quiet. He sat up for a moment before letting himself fall back again with a sigh. He buried his face into the pillow and pulled the covers up over his ears.

He drifted off, the national anthem faded away. They're arguing again, he thought, but I'm no longer going to let it bother me. I'm not a child any more. He resolved not to dwell on it, and indeed, within seconds he managed to turn his thoughts to other matters: Uncle Robert, Aunt Lise, the as-yet-unknown lady with the exotic name, Mrs R. Mexocos. A Hispanic woman probably, there were notes of Mexico, Texas, Texaco. Was she old or young? Young probably. On Saturday he'd find out.

But again he heard his parents' voices, louder now. He snorted furiously, realising that sleep was futile for the time being. Let me stay calm, he told himself. It's nothing unusual. My parents are arguing, they don't belong together, a failed marriage. I'm the product of a failed marriage, he thought, not without self-pity. Two years earlier (or was it three already?), he'd had to admit for the first time that things were not quite right between his parents. It was also nighttime, also a spring night. He was lying awake just as now, in the same room and the same bed. He'd woken up and heard his mother crying. It had affected him deeply. It had affected him so deeply that he had almost cried, he probably had cried. His mother lay sobbing in the middle of the night and his world, a magnificent edifice composed of the sweet thoughts of a thirteen-year-old lad, had shattered. What was he to believe in now? He had pictured his mother, curled up in a ball in the big double bed, venting her grievances about her failed marriage to her grown-up daughter. During that period his father was on a lengthy business trip and the reason for this nocturnal drama was that he'd barely been in touch at all. He heard Cora Alide's voice reassuring her periodically. But each time, his mother burst into tears again, spitting out in crumbling words everything she must have kept bottled up. We should have called it a day ages ago, she sobbed, but that man was always against it.

That man was his father, an essentially friendly man, who was only a little forgetful and had many cares which his wife had no idea of. That night Karel's room was filled with grief. The grief that seemed to go with having a heart. He'd wanted to shout: shut up, shut up, admit that you're lying. But he lay still, staring into the darkness, having fragmented thoughts about books in which boys ran away to sea. He'd wanted to get out of bed and console his mother, say that she'd misjudged his father, that he was a good man, a man he loved a lot. He wanted to say that he loved her just as much, because they belonged together, an inseparable pair, an eternal embrace on a timeless photograph. But he continued to lie there, his ear to the wall, his eyes wide open, thinking that 'a great sea change' was coming into his life. And he started blaming himself, promising he'd be nicer to his parents, he'd try harder at school. But again his mother cried in a choked-up voice that her life was no longer worth living. And then Cora Alide began to sob too, even though she was a full twenty years old.

He'd fallen asleep with his fingers in his ears, projecting with grim determination the old photograph of his newly engaged parents into his mind: his mother with a plump face and bouncy hair, gazing up happily at his father, a young man with a long neck, a small moustache and pale eyes. Whose fault was it? Whose fault was it? he'd wondered, over and over, before falling asleep.

Now, too, Karel fell asleep but this time he was more angry than sad. The anger was still in him when, after a relatively short time, he woke up again with a strong urge to urinate. It was a quarter to four. He lay in bed a little longer, not able to face the chilly corridor, telling himself he could hang on. He lay like this a few minutes longer, his belly hard and tense. His parents were still talking but they were calmer now and there was a hum in the air.

Karel threw off his covers and felt for his slippers, which he couldn't find. Grumbling, he walked barefoot across the cold linoleum floor in the hallway. Swaying slightly, he relieved himself and stared out of the toilet window at the clear starry sky. But not just stars, there were also broad beams of white light, which jerked back and forth. And the steady buzz continued. Karel inhaled deeply and stood motionlessly at the window.

'Is that you, Karel?' he heard his brother's voice say.

'Yes,' he replied.

'The war is here,' his brother said.

'War?' he queried.

'Yes,' said his brother, who was standing, fully dressed, in the doorway to their parents' bedroom. Karel, overcome by a fit of shivers, went in to them. His mother lay in bed, her hair up, her face small and shiny. His father was standing at the window, half dressed, his braces over his pyjama top. His brother was smoking a cigarette.

'The Germans have invaded,' his mother said.

'The bastards,' his father said, and began taking off his trousers again.

'What are you going to do?' Mrs Ruis asked.

'Sleep,' his father replied brusquely.

'But we're at war, Father,' his mother said in an insistent tone as though she were speaking to a deaf person.

'So what?' his father said, getting into bed. 'Is that a reason for me not to sleep? Will it help anyone if I stand at the window getting wound up? It's not like that'll stop the Germans. Goodnight.' He switched off the light. There was a rumbling in the distance now, as though a storm were on its way.

4

THERE'S A WAR ON and my father's gone to sleep, thought the boy. My father doesn't have to do anything, he doesn't have to go anywhere, he doesn't have to put on a helmet, he doesn't have to put on boots, or report for duty on a public square saying, 'Here I am, ready to defend our fatherland.'

He was wide awake now and quickly got fully dressed, though he didn't wash. The streetlights were shining like nothing had happened. What had happened though? He didn't know. How many soldiers were already dead?

Day was already breaking and the humming became louder. Karel clumped around the slumbering house. I ought to have cleaned my teeth at any rate, he thought. A chill came over him. His brother was standing on the balcony, his face as white as a sheet. Philip Lodewijk Robert greeted Karel in a serious tone; Karel responded in an equally serious tone and joined him. There were shadowy figures on almost all of the balconies, most of them wearing hastily thrown together outfits or faded dressing gowns. They were talking to each other in hushed tones as though it were forbidden to speak loudly. Their voices rustled like dead rushes. Nobody laughed.

Karel wondered what all the people were looking at. A soldier raced past on a ladies' bike and there was a lull in the talking. After that a milk truck drove past, churns clattering, a white flag waved from the driver's cabin. MILK IS FOR ALL, BIG AND SMALL was written on the back.

Karel's brother went inside to make a strong pot of coffee. When Karel took his cup, he realised his hands were shaking. His brother gave him a cigarette. He leaned over the balcony railings, smoking. It was almost light now and the houses on the other side of the street were crested with pink. The female spectators vanished from the balconies and the voices became louder.

Doom has befallen us, thought Karel, not without satisfaction. His nerves were akin to those on the night before his birthday. There was a pleasant queasiness in his stomach. It was as though a hitherto unknown recording device had been triggered inside his head, something like an extra sense. A bracing shower of patriotism and fear appeared to have rained down on his street. Here and there flags had been hung out as though it were Queen's Day. Nervous new sounds tripped from the radio, populating the room like rats. Heinkel, Junker, Messerschmitt, Messerschmitt *numero* twelve. War was now more than a monotone hum and rattling in the distance, it was also pink glittering dots in a V-formation in a bright blue sky, dots bearing the names of German millionaires.

'German troops crossed the Dutch border last night and have engaged with our border forces. Our border forces are carrying out their assigned task…'

From all the windows, the loudspeaker voice bellowed through the street. Down all the streets. The entire city. The entire country. The Netherlands is at war with Germany. How would an adult respond to these terrible tidings, he wondered? I want to laugh, jump around, run out onto the street. But what would an adult want to do?

Karel Ruis stood on the balcony without moving; bags under his eyes and an unwashed face, a boy of seventeen, who had got overexcited and hadn't slept enough. He pictured a map of the country. The map of my fatherland, he thought, a grassy green map. Germany, our eastern neighbour, is pale pink. How does that work, crossing a border? What does it look like? There's a border crossing with two barriers, one red-and-white one, the other red and black, I think, and a strip of no-man's-land between them and on either side, two sentry posts. There are two soldiers in those little watchhouses, they're wearing long coats and have rifles balanced upright at their feet. One of them has bound his lower legs in green strips of cloth, the other is wearing ankle-high boots. One Dutch soldier, one German soldier. They can see each other standing there. But now the Germans cross our border. Do they take that same route then? Do they drive right through the red-and-white barrier in an armoured car, after shooting the Dutch soldier? Is he suddenly shot down by his fellow from fifty feet away, whom he regularly ran into on his patrol and maybe said *Guten Abend* to sometimes? Alright, so they cross the border in one of those armoured cars and after that the soldiers get into that infantryman position where they're leaning forward, fingers on triggers. So they do all this quietly or do they make a lot of noise? Those armoured cars chug quite loudly, of course. This is likely to alert the Dutch soldiers lying in position a little further along. Others are asleep in their beds in requisitioned houses. Suddenly the sirens go off. The Germans are at the door, and then you have to calmly bind those strips around your legs. Some buttons are pressed and bombs fall on the roads and a couple of bridges explode into the air. They carry out their assigned task. And this happens in other places, too, of course. Everywhere Germans are crossing that red dotted line between pale pink and grassy green, not just on the roads, but often in the woods or fields. They creep through the cornfields, their helmets pulled down over their eyes like sun visors.

'Only to the east of Arnhem, around fifteen kilometres from the Dutch–German border, have the Germans advanced as far as the IJssel…'

'To all intents and appearances, my wish has come true,' Karel slowly told himself. Slowly, as though he had trouble formulating this absurd observation that had been reverberating at the back of his mind for some time, trouble formulating it in reasonable language without doing himself harm. War has come, he thought. The dictator is standing on his balcony, resting his fists on the balustrade. Yesterday afternoon, two steps behind him at his desk, he issued a series of death sentences, without defence or witnesses, solely on the grounds of moral certainty. Today the executions will begin.

He stared nervously at the planes which were still flying over in orderly constellations, paying no heed to the sparse puffs of smoke that tried in vain to sow confusion in their more advanced mathematics.

What was he going to do with Uncle Robert's letter now? he thought, but this was immediately subsumed by a new thought: It's good to have a fatherland. And then, apparently as a musical accompaniment to the news on the radio, somebody began to hammer out the national anthem on the piano, the music reverberating with copious pedal work and baroque embellishments. The notes leaped into the houses like saluting soldiers. The people on the street and the balconies stood up straight. Some men tipped their hats.

Their ironic neighbour had also appeared on his balcony.

'*Guten Morgen,*' he joked to Karel. 'It has come to this – *es ist so weit.*' He smiled grimly. He was a small, crumpled man.

'The English will be here soon,' he said. 'It will be alright. Where is your father though?'

'He's asleep,' said Karel.

'Good lord,' said the neighbour, 'Mr Ruis is asleep.' He began to sing a German lullaby in a mocking tone, '*Schlafe, mein Prinzchen, schlaf ein…*'

5

The sitting room was still filled with the ridiculous air of peacetime. Karel's parents appeared unusually early, at half past seven that morning. They roamed around the room uneasily. His father's brick-red jaw was clean-shaven. He took an atlas from the bookshelf and searched for place names, which his sons read out loud in turn, like passwords. 'Only a hundred kilometres from here,' he sniffed and started pacing back and forth. Mrs Ruis sat down on the sofa, her hands idle on her knees, a duster on her lap. Her thin hair fell in waves onto her forehead. She gazed around in astonishment. Her husband sat down next to her and now the two parents sat side by side on the sofa, reading the morning newspaper with dejected expressions on their faces.

'All educational establishments will be closed until further notice,' Mrs Ruis said. 'Parents are requested to keep their children at home.'

Breakfast was something of an event, since it was rare for the whole family to sit down to it together. It might happen on a very special occasion like a birthday or before they set off on holiday.

This was a meal that should be preceded by a prayer, thought Karel, or at any rate some words of encouragement. He looked at his father. His father said, 'The Germans are strong. They're incredibly strong.' In his absent-mindedness he didn't put slivers of cheese on his bread but extra-thick slices. He got up to leave for the office and kissed his wife on her pale ears, first a cautious kiss on the left one, then a cautious kiss on the right. Their children watched in silence. He said, 'I'll be home soon, Cora. You all must be brave.' After that he shook his children by the hand, one by one. Karel was last.

You all must be brave, the boy repeated to himself. The room was perfectly quiet. He looked at the breakfast table laid with cheese, jam, spiced bread, the teacups. The balcony doors were still open. Outside spring was steaming, the milkman was serving his customers and a flower-seller was loudly extolling his potted ferns.

Karel's brother said, 'I'm off to join the home guard. There was an appeal for volunteers in the paper. I want to do something. I want to do something at least, otherwise I'll go mad.'

He wants to do something, thought Karel, but last year he didn't eat or sleep for almost a whole week so that he'd be turned down for military service. And he managed it, but now he wants to do something otherwise he'll go mad. Karel saw his father disappearing into the distance, a man with long sticks for legs and an attaché case.

Not long afterwards, Karel left the house too. 'I'm going to see whether anything's happening at school,' he told his mother. But once outdoors, he headed towards the city centre. In his pocket he had the ten-guilder note as well as Uncle Robert's note for Mrs Mexocos. He didn't take the tram but ambled through the busy shopping streets. He divided his immediate attention between all the alluring girls he came across and himself. But the thought that war had come was constantly on his mind. He searched for clues but his gaze repeatedly wandered back to his own reflection in the shop windows. He had put on the trousers of his dark-blue suit (his first and only pair of long trousers), a lightweight summer coat, a brightly coloured checked shirt and a plain grey tie. The shirt was actually part of his camping outfit, but with this particular combination he felt it lent him a modern, artistic air.

Men in overalls were busy piling sandbags in front of the ground-floor windows of some of the buildings. The police were wearing blue soldier's helmets and everywhere he looked there were civilian patrols dressed in ochre-coloured uniforms and bearing long, old-fashioned rifles. Karel didn't see any real soldiers anywhere. No planes had flown over for several hours and the shooting had stopped too. Karel was sorely disappointed that very little of note was happening. There were cars on the roads, the shops were open and the people didn't look any sadder or happier than usual. It seemed slightly busier on the streets, that was all.

In the newspaper district, hundreds of people were standing in front of the bulletin boards reading the latest news. The murmur of their voices hung like a low storm cloud over their heads; it was interspersed with the nervous lightning energy of the mounted police who barked that gatherings were forbidden. But the people didn't listen to the mounted officers and mutteringly took in the latest news.

'French and British tanks and motorised troops have crossed the Belgian border. They were met by grateful Belgians bearing flowers and beer,' Karel read. He drifted onwards.

The outdoor cafés were packed. Charming ladies wearing sunglasses lounged in their chairs, enjoying the sun. Karel wished he dared take a seat too. The clock struck half past nine. He bought an ice cream from a cart. 'Some Brits have already arrived at the train station,' the ice-cream vendor said. Karel walked onto the square in front of the station, licking his ice cream. His attention was drawn by a jeering crowd. A small man was being escorted by two civilian guards. The man was unshaven, wore a beret and no shirt collar. He stared at the ground as they walked him along and put up no resistance. The guards gripped his upper arms tightly, causing them to stick out to the side like broken wings. The collar of his jacket was pulled up to his ears. A whole line of people followed him, shouting, 'Traitor! Filthy traitor!' The same words again and again in a whiny, almost impassive tone. Karel walked along with them for a short distance, thinking that some shocking wartime action would follow now, but he didn't join in with the chorus of voices. In the end he stopped and watched the group go, until a man, not in uniform but with a band around his arm, commanded him to move on.

He circumnavigated the station, keeping his eyes peeled for any soldiers in khaki, but there was nothing special to see. Trains puffed in and out of the station and rail workers in blue smocks walked around with copper klaxons. An ocean liner headed out to sea over the wide river, pulled by two yapping tugboats. A Dutch flag hung from its mast.

Karel sat down on a bollard on the quayside and looked out across the gleaming water. He began to reflect. I'm looking out across the harbour, he thought. It's the first morning of the war and I'm looking out across the harbour. Where is the war? It's a beautiful, clear spring day. The river smells salty. The view is genuinely stunning: a typically Dutch riverscape. Plumes of smoke from the factories on the facing bank. But the fascists have crossed our border. This lovely weather is useless. It's inappropriate. It's misleading for everyone, it should be raining. There should be rain falling over this riverscape. It should really be cold and gloomy.

He felt a little disappointed, almost cheated. Boats and shunting trains, as though nothing had happened. And as he turned into one of the lanes by the harbour, a thought wouldn't let him be: *it's as though nothing has happened.* When I get home later everyone will be sitting at the table like normal. It's the school holidays. Nothing has happened at all. My mother will say, 'Why are you so late? Your fried egg is cold.' I'll reply, 'I went for a walk.' 'Did something happen?' Mum will ask. And I'll reply, 'No, nothing happened.' And I'll be jealous of my father because he gets two fried eggs and I only get one. He gets two fried eggs because he's a father. First he cuts away the whites, then he downs the yolks in a single gulp. That's how my father eats fried eggs. Afterwards there are little yellow crusty bits at the corners of his mouth. And my mother will say, 'Wipe your mouth, Father!'

Karel Ruis walked along the narrow lane. Bars were clustered side by side, their doors stood wide open and green curtains billowed out, casting foul breath across the tarmac. Girls with puffed-out blond hair and shiny black skirts were beating carpets.

Karel knew this neighbourhood reasonably well. Not infrequently he'd cycle here of an evening with a group of classmates to giggle and shudder at the painted ladies in the red-lit windows. It was an incredibly exciting neighbourhood which offered lots of things to dream about in bed. The water in the canal was feculent and dead. The footsteps of slinking gentlemen scuffed across the rickety bridges. Cigarettes glowed at the street corners and there was a strange, medicinal, peppery smell.

But now it was quiet and sunny. The daylight disarmed Karel Ruis. The women sat peacefully on their doorsteps, needlework on their laps. The church bells issued a rousing patriotic anthem, 'Merck toch hoe sterck'. See how strong and valiant we are! The women barely glanced at Karel as he passed and didn't call out to him. Only one of them gave him a quiet wink and lifted her skirt above her knee. Die, he thought. She was a pale chubby woman in a petticoat. He hurried past intently and heard her lisping behind his back. I'm a seventeen-year-old boy, he thought. In Germany you have to become a soldier at that age, but that woman is fifty at least. That woman must be just as old as Aunt Lise, only fatter.

A steady buzzing began to fill his ears. The buzzing quickly got louder. He jerked to a halt and looked up. As his gaze swept upward, he saw the woman smiling at him and then suddenly she threw her head back and looked up too. Two planes flew over the city, two silver planes. They swooped so smoothly, so quickly and gently that Karel forgot the noise. They were right above him now. Karel saw two dots falling, he saw the bombs falling and heard a high-pitched wail. He lowered his head and suffered the prostitute's gurgling screams. She opened her fleshy arms, her fingers spread, her belly was fat and round. Karel Ruis didn't think of dying. He listened, astonished, to the bombs falling. Afterwards there was only dust and the stately wail of the sirens. The bomb has fallen, he thought, the bomb has fallen, the bomb has fallen – as though he were memorising a key phrase for an exam.

He stood among dozens of warm bodies in an air-raid shelter, thinking: you can't cry about this any more, crying is pointless. The sirens stopped and there was a hush outside as though it had snowed. The huddle of people said nothing and trembled collectively. Most of them were women, some were still clutching their knitting. The chubby woman stood gasping for breath, her face pale and puffy, gasping for breath through a clown's mouth, nothing else. She was still alive. A spindly blond woman muttered with closed eyes, she was probably praying to God. A man from the air-raid defence entered, dusty, his helmet tilted back on his head. He said something and everyone started whispering. They whispered two names: Annie and Neel, Annie and Neel.

A while later the all clear was sounded and everyone was allowed to go back into the sunlight and continue with their daily business. Karel saw that two houses which he'd walked past on his way had been blown up. The other bomb had apparently landed in the canal, and the fronts of at least ten houses were covered in a thick layer of sludge. The stench was suffocating. In the middle of the street there was a bed, practically intact. You could go and lie down in it, pull the covers over your head and think: let them get on with it, let them get on with it, I'm not here, I'm asleep.

6

KAREL RUIS WALKED THROUGH THE PARK. His eyes took in flowerbeds, swans and children, but his mind said: this is only the start. I didn't even see the dead people; I saw the living people, the survivors. I'm a survivor myself, but nobody knows, nobody can see it on me.

He gazed around. He was walking through the park. He'd hidden from the park keeper along this little path, he'd skated on this pond, in this park he'd collected chestnuts, on this bench he'd had to keep his hands to himself. His mother had pushed him around this park in his pram and had him photographed wearing a ludicrous hat and holding a letter.

That was all in the past now, this park and everything he'd experienced there, was in the past. It no longer existed, it had become a memory. The only thing that still existed were the bombed houses.

He looked at his dust-covered shoes and began to wipe them with a handful of grass. He'd already walked halfway around the park, almost at a trot, as though he had to be somewhere punctually and he was already running late. It wasn't even midday, though, and school had broken up. He repeatedly filled his mouth at an isolated drinking fountain, but the claggy taste of sleep refused to be spat out. The fresh greenery looked dull to him, as though he were viewing it through tinted spectacles and it was covered in a sad blue haze.

He slowly began to head homewards. Some people had stuck strips of gummed paper over their windows. A little further along, painters were busy doing up a row of houses. An older painter with a beard was applying a name to a newly varnished door with contrived flourishes: R.P. KRAMARSK.

Two negatives are being superimposed, he thought, two clock mechanisms are marking different times. All kinds of things are happening and nothing is happening. The bomb has fallen and I'm the only one who knows. I wanted to stare at those women and a bomb fell. Yesterday I said, 'Fall, bomb, fall!', and today it fell. And trees fell, people fell, houses fell. Dear Lord, he thought, they're having their names put on their doors in curly letters. They're having their front walls daubed in cream-coloured paint to make them look fancy and stop them decaying. But other housefronts are covered in sludge, thick stinking sludge.

Every second I spend loitering here, Dutch soldiers are falling, and falling means dying, dying like that run-over girl, they're falling for their fatherland (why else would you?), for our fatherland, my fatherland, father- and motherland, my father and mother. My cousin who is a medical officer is cutting bullets from living flesh now. Dutch bullets and German bullets, Dutch flesh and German flesh. He's amputating legs non-stop, legs of two nationalities. And I'm just walking around. I stroll around the harbour and I get a feeling in the pit of my stomach. I listen to the national anthem and I get a feeling in the pit of my stomach.

Karel Ruis felt lonely. The loneliness crept over him like cold mist. He thought back to the wonderful shiver that had tickled his spine and spread a pleasant warmth through his intestines that morning when he'd heard the national anthem. Who'd felt lonely then? The birds cheeped and the national anthem was played and it was all satisfying and good and fair, it had felt physically satisfying and good and fair. A justified war, we are in the right. My nation is in the right.

He touched his face furtively. A rudimentary moustache. He touched his eyes, his ears, his nose. I'm seventeen years old, he thought. Sweet seventeen, and I wanted to see those ruddy stupid women sitting at those windows and heaven sent a bomb to warn me of sin.

His mother opened the door from above and shouted down, 'Is that you, Karel?' Her voice tumbled down the steep staircase nervously. He didn't see the need to reply but stepped indoors. 'Thank God,' said his mother. 'A weight off my mind. You mustn't go out alone any more. Anything could happen now, son.'

He had to agree with her: anything could happen. But it could happen everywhere. Here and on the other side of the street and in the city centre and in the park. It happened in stages. This was just the start. You could no longer take your life for granted. You could no longer take your life for granted wherever you were.

He collapsed into a chair. He opened his eyes wide as though he were trying his hardest to stay awake. His brother was a silhouette at the window. A silhouette busy sticking gummed paper over the panes, diamond-shaped, a kind of makeshift stained glass. There was a bowl of water and a sponge next to him and he used this to carefully dampen each strip of paper. A large cigar hung from his mouth. On the radio a man was talking about blackouts, a man with a dull voice which reminded Karel of his history teacher's. His brother turned to him, 'Any news?' he asked.

'What happened to you?' Karel responded.

'I got a haircut,' his brother said.

'Yes, I can see that,' said Karel. 'But it's much too short. You look like an idiot. Why did you get your hair cut?'

'I applied to the home guard and they told me I'd never be taken on with such long hair,' his brother explained.

'And did they take you on?' Karel asked.

'Yes, they took me on,' said his brother, 'after I promised to have my hair cut. They gave me a registration number.' He showed Karel a letter with the number 13186. 'I'll get a call-up soon,' he said. He took the cigar from his mouth and pulled off a strip of paper that was crooked. After that he tried to comb his hair, which was only two centimetres long.

'A bomb fell in the centre. What a bang it made!' he said.

'Yes, a terrible bang,' said Karel.

'Have you heard anything about it?' his brother asked. 'Like where it landed?'

'I don't know,' said Karel. 'No one's told me anything.'

7

THE FOLLOWING AFTERNOON Karel went to Mrs Mexocos's house to deliver the letter. Mrs Mexocos lived in the wasteland of new houses on the edge of the city, a windy neighbourhood that Karel knew only by name. It was very close to the viaduct which a train to Uncle Robert's town rattled over every half hour. It must be strangely exciting to ride right past your own street on a train, thought Karel. There were children whooping and playing hopscotch all over the place and sand blew across the pavements. Down every side street you caught a glimpse of shared gardens with wigwams made of old planks and tar paper. A neighbourhood that made you feel desolate and lonely. For a brief instant, Karel considered just chucking the letter in the letterbox and forgetting all about Mrs Mexocos. But then he heard a train passing and he rang the bell. The door opened with a hiss. He began to climb four flights of stairs. On the top floor, a girl of his own age stood in the doorway. The girl was small of stature but had a wise, round face. Her hair was long and black. She was dressed in a very ladylike fashion in a black velvet dress. She was in the process of drinking a bottle of lemonade through a straw.

'Does Mrs Mexocos live here?' he asked.

The girl nodded without taking the straw from her mouth.

'I've brought a letter,' he said, taking it out of his pocket.

After she'd carefully sucked the last drops of lemonade from the bottle, the girl said, 'Give it here.'

'I'm to wait for a reply,' he said. 'Are you Mrs Mexocos?'

The girl began to laugh. 'What makes you think that?' she asked. 'She's my mother. Do you need to speak to her? Do you have a letter of recommendation? Are you a model? I'll call her, come inside.'

Karel entered a small hallway which smelled of eau de Cologne. On the walls there were pictures made of green and red wool. One depicted a fish, a monstrous fish with large green scales and red fins and eyes.

'Who is it, Ria?' a female voice enquired.

'A boy who wants to speak to you,' said the girl. 'A life model, I think.'

'But it's hardly the time for models now!' said the voice.

'I've come to deliver a letter,' said Karel, 'and I'm supposed to wait for a reply.'

'He's come to bring a letter and he is supposed to wait for a reply,' said Ria.

'Show him into the drawing room,' said the voice.

Ria took him to a room where all the furniture was white. The chairs were made of wicker and a wooden doll hung above the mantelpiece, a kind of harlequin, pale pink and pale green. There was a white grand piano in front of the window.

'Take a seat,' the girl said casually. Aside from this, she ignored Karel. She started brushing her black hair with a metal hairbrush. Karel saw that there was a portrait photograph on top of the piano in a dark lacquer frame. The photo was the only old-fashioned thing in the room. It was of a man with a mad hairdo and a moustache, a man who sat at a piano with his hands on the keys, his head proudly raised. It was a portrait of Uncle Robert. Karel couldn't help feeling that the picture was out of place in this room, it was as though it had just washed up there somehow.

He noticed that his fingernails were dirty and his smart blue trousers had begun to lose their crease. Uncle Robert's worldly appearance did not put him at ease. Ria had sat down at the piano and began to play. She began to play shrill jazz music and peered intently at the sheet music in front of her, which was covered in notes. It was apparently very difficult because she looked almost aggrieved and stamped her foot every time she played a wrong note.

The door opened and her mother came in. Mrs Mexocos was wearing a bathing suit. She was a very tall lady. Her hair was greying but apart from that she looked very young. She had a soft, round face and her mouth was half-open. Her skin was smooth and brown. Karel immediately thought of summer, a warm, fragrant summer holiday without war, a beach with happy suntanned people, of whom Mrs Mexocos was one, a beautiful mother in a scarlet bathing suit, lying stretched out in the hot sand. What a mother! he thought.

Mrs Mexocos walked towards him with raised hands. She said, 'Please forgive me for keeping you waiting for so long. We've just moved in and I'm still in disarray. Look out, my hands are very dirty.' She offered Karel a sinewy wrist and he wrapped his fingers briefly around her bracelet made of bone.

'My name is Karel Ruis,' he said, 'I've brought you a letter from my uncle Robert. Uncle Robert asked—'

'Oh!' said Mrs Mexocos, reaching a dirty hand for the letter. She tore it open and walked to the mantelpiece as she read it. She leaned against the mantelpiece, right in front of the grinning harlequin, which peered out from behind her bare shoulder. Mrs Mexocos read the letter from start to finish several times and appeared to be thinking deeply.

Ria had stopped playing and was now studying Karel. She regarded him intently but didn't smile. She picked a cigarette from a case with her shiny purple fingernails and stuck it between her pursed lips. 'Smoke?' she asked Karel. She tossed him a cigarette and leaned back in her chair, her legs crossed, a small woman wearing silk stockings. She waited for a light; she waited very patiently until he realised what she was waiting for. He hastily struck a match and walked over to her holding it. He had to cross the whole room and by the time he could finally offer her the flame, he felt his nails scorching.

'Ouch?' she said.

'No,' said Karel.

He looked closely at her eyes, which were green, buttonhole slits, and not particularly pretty at all. 'Thank you,' she said, and the tone in which she said it was so unattainable that Karel wondered whether he wouldn't fall in love with the girl on the spot.

Her mother rolled the letter into a cylinder which she pensively stuck under the shoulder strap of her bathing suit. 'Hmm, I don't know,' she said to Karel. Then she asked with a puzzled face, 'Did you say you were supposed to wait for a reply?'

'Well, a reply of sorts,' he said. 'Uncle Robert asked me to bring this letter to you and said you'd give me a letter for him and I wasn't to speak of the matter to anybody.'

'Good old Robert,' said Mrs Mexocos. 'Are you fond of your uncle?' she asked. 'Do you drink at all? Would you like a tipple?'

'Oh, I do,' said Karel. 'Yes please, ma'am,' he said.

'Robert's nephew called you ma'am,' giggled Ria, as she went over to the cabinet. 'Jenever or sherry?' she asked.

'My name is Ria,' said Mrs Mexocos. 'I'm called Ria, just like my daughter. Feel free to call me Ria.'

'Jenever or sherry?' the daughter repeated.

'Sherry, if I may,' said Karel.

The three of them sat around a low glass-topped table. Beneath the glass was a picture of fierce-looking horsemen in a snowy landscape. Mrs Mexocos lounged in a deep chair, her bare legs stretched out in front of her. She had on shoes with rope soles, fastened with ribbons crossed all the way up her calves. The two Rias briefly raised their glasses chest-high and said, 'Cheers!' Karel did the same. The sherry tasted bitter.

'Your uncle Robert writes that he's had a serious talk with you,' mother Ria said. '*I've informed him*, he wrote. What did he tell you?' She smiled expectantly and laid a finger against her large nose.

What did he tell me? Karel thought in confusion. He looked at the mother's long legs and the silk stockings and elegant shoes worn by her daughter. Have I been informed of something? he wondered.

He replied, 'Yes, he had a serious talk with me. He asked me whether I knew why he had such a cheerful disposition despite all the misfortunes he's suffered. I said no. And then he said he'd tell me how that came about. He said it was because there was a great joy in his life. But he never got on to what that joy was because Aunt Lise entered the room. He just managed to give me that letter but he didn't explain.'

'I'm sure he will tell you,' said Mrs Mexocos in a laughing tone of reassurance as she raised her glass.

'We have a lovely portrait of your uncle Robert,' her daughter said.

'Yes,' said Karel, pointing at the piano. 'I've seen it.'

'No, that's an old one. I mean the portrait that my mother made recently. It's a much better likeness than that photograph. Would you like to see it, Karel?'

She called me Karel, he thought gleefully. She'd jumped to her feet and now led the way. Her cigarette dangled from her lips. She looked back at him a couple of times as though she wanted to make sure he was actually following her. He was more than happy to follow her!

They walked down the hall and entered a room. It was filled with boxes and crates, and in the middle there was a wonderfully broad double bed, covered in all sorts of shoes and clothes. There were mainly shoes, shoes of every conceivable style and shape: gold-leather sandals, raffia mules, boudoir slippers and even hiking boots.

Little Ria ducked under the bed and pulled out an enormous canvas. She propped it up against the wall. 'This is it,' she said.

Karel looked at the portrait of his uncle. It was entirely composed of stuck-on scraps of fabric. The bald head was represented by a patch of shiny pink lingerie. The eyes were big, much too big, bright-blue frayed linen with little white flowers; its frayed edges were the eyelashes. Uncle Robert gazed at his nephew kindly and thoughtfully, with an expression on his patchwork face that was entirely new to Karel. His lips and ears were made of thick red felt and his cheeks of a natural-coloured shantung silk. His torso was naked and shiny pink too, and below it was a loincloth which was just an ordinary towel, a kitchen hand-towel, blue and grey checked.

'Don't you think it's pretty?' Ria said.

'Yes, I think it's very pretty,' said Karel. 'The strange thing is, it looks just like him.'

'That's not strange at all,' said Ria. 'My mother is a great artist. She's a ballet dancer too and she designs shoes and draws life models,' she said.

'Life models?' Karel asked.

'Yes,' said Ria, 'she likes drawing nudes. She likes naked bodies. Particularly male bodies, young male bodies. I can understand that,' she said.

Mrs Mexocos came into the room on her long legs. She washed her hands in a basin. 'What a mess,' she said as though she hadn't seen it before. 'What am I to do with all this now?' she asked. But nobody replied. She took a few dance steps, her head thrown back, her arms raised elegantly above her. She stood like this for a while, tilted from the waist.

FALL, BOMB, FALL

As she danced she asked, 'Is there any news? Have the English arrived already?'

'I don't know,' said Karel, 'but they're sure to come.'

'I hope so, I hope so,' said Mrs Mexocos, 'otherwise it's not looking pretty.'

'Yes,' said Karel, thinking: what will happen if the English don't come?

'We have low expectations of the Germans,' said Mrs Mexocos. She took a pot of skin cream from under the bed and began to rub it on her hands. 'We are Jewish,' said Mrs Mexocos. 'Jewish people have the lowest expectations of Germans. The Germans are killing Jewish people like cattle. I don't know how many of my German friends they've already killed. If the Germans come,' she said, 'we'll have to flee. And I think they will come, the Germans. All day I've been thinking, why should I deal with that mess, what's the point of it now? Next month I'll be in America. Or a concentration camp. Yes, Robert was right, we should have left long ago. Let's have another glass of sherry,' she said.

They drank sherry. Large brimming glasses of it. Karel said, 'You're being pessimistic, Ria, you're being pessimistic. Why wouldn't the English come? We're their allies now. The Germans will never get further than our defensive waterline when it's flooded. Everyone knows that. It's in all the papers. The Germans have never won a war.'

'No,' said mother Ria, pouring Karel another large, brimming glass. 'But maybe they'll win this war. And even if they lose in the end, they can do us a lot of damage beforehand.'

Karel didn't understand how he could ever have found the sherry bitter. A great warmth churned behind his ribcage. The horsemen chased through the snowstorm under his glass. The room was white and lovely, the patchwork pictures were lovely, the two Rias were lovely. How nice it would be to live in such a room, he thought, to be able to live here, he thought. The idea that the two Rias might have to flee this paradise because of the mad whims of the German dictator infuriated him. He wanted to say something nice and he said, 'It's lovely here. It would be wonderful to live here with you.'

The mother and daughter didn't laugh at him but looked at him with their friendly brown and green eyes. Little Ria said, 'You're always welcome.'

After that she sat down at the piano and played a slow, jolting melody. Karel got the urge to shut his eyes. When it was over he thought: so this is the music you need to hate in order to love Beethoven. But I hate Beethoven and this music is the nicest I've ever heard. He easily could have melted now, but he didn't and he was overcome by a warm, trembling feeling, as though tears were welling up inside. A bomb has fallen, he thought, but what does it matter? Hello war, he said to himself. In the distance he heard a train rattle over the viaduct. Suddenly he said, 'What time is it?'

'I don't know exactly,' said Mrs Mexocos apathetically, 'around six?' But it turned out to be already half past.

'I have to go,' said Karel, 'we eat dinner at six!' He got to his feet with breezy haste. 'Oh, the letter, the letter for Uncle Robert,' he said.

'That'll have to wait until tomorrow,' said Mrs Mexocos. 'I can't write it now. Could you drop round again tomorrow afternoon?'

'Yes, come tomorrow afternoon,' said Little Ria, 'we can take a walk together.'

8

THE NEXT DAY WAS A SUNDAY, an unusual Sunday because everyone was up early. Karel's brother had bought a large map of the Netherlands and little paper flags on pins, twenty red-white-and-blue and twenty with swastikas. He still hadn't been called up by the civil defence corps but wanted to mark out the frontline in preparation.

He said, 'I need a clear idea of how far they've advanced. I need to be able to picture it exactly.' He studied the morning newspapers, but the army reports were so vague he didn't know what to do with his flags. There were almost no place-names in the army reports. He'd spread the map out on the table and he and their father hunched over it, worried, resting their weight on their knuckles as though they were posing for a photograph. 'Philip Lodewijk Robert and his Field Marshal Ruis at headquarters. These men are charged with a difficult task.'

Karel's mother was sitting by the radio with Cora Alide. A clergyman was preaching, 'I have sunk into the miry depths, where there is no footing; I have drifted into deep waters, where the flood engulfs me. I am weary from my crying; my throat is parched. My eyes fail, looking for my God.' Karel thought of the soldiers lying in the trenches along the IJssel line of defence. Church bells were ringing everywhere. At half past twelve he got to his feet, ambled to the door and said, 'I'm going for a ride on my bike.'

'Be careful,' said his mother. 'Don't be back as late as you were yesterday. We're going to have dinner at half past five.'

His father said, 'Enjoy yourself, lad.'

Cora Alide said, 'Send her my regards. Is she sweet?'

Karel whistled as he got out his bike. My parents are surely saying how immature I am, he thought, *the seriousness of the situation has completely passed the child by.* He chuckled. Enjoy yourself and be careful. Did they even know what they meant by this? He pictured them sitting in their tidy brown sitting room, a hotel room, their life was a hotel room between two wars. What did he even have in common with these people? They weren't big, they weren't small, they lived off a salary and they weren't that old yet and they suffered. But why did they suffer? I eat their tinned salmon sandwiches, he thought, and they taste nice, but I'm growing out from under their hands, our paths are diverging. I'm lying in a boat, bobbing between the two Rias, I'm lying stock-still. Their eyes are green and brown. Uncle Robert turns up with provisions. A desert island and I'm lying deathly still and they bring me to life – drinking sherry and eating croquettes on the dictator's grave.

Karel Ruis cycled at a leisurely pace through the car-less streets, where families were walking along in reciprocal boredom. There were no sporting events and the trains departed irregularly. People went about their business with worried expressions and cake boxes and read special supplements and kept all their silver coins in their pockets. Organ music issued from a church. An organist expressed with joyous conviction that he had put his faith in the Lord; the organ's bass notes growled like bombers in the spring skies, soaring up to the fleecy clouds in search of heaven's gates.

The previous day and night it had remained calm in and above the city – planes flew over, but the gunfire had stopped. It was quite possible that the entire city might start celebrating soon, 'Hoorah! A truce has been called!' *Germany has surrendered! The Treaty of Mill has been signed – in an old Dutch windmill in the tiny village of Mill, the treaty was signed by...* But the city remained anxiously quiet, only in its bars was there a little bragging, people were saying, 'The Germans may have crossed the IJssel river to the east of Arnhem but the French and the Brits are already in Brabant.'

He bought a bunch of ox-eye daisies from a flower-seller in front of a hospital. They were incredibly strong flowers, the vendor told him, these flowers weren't at all bothered by a bit of chloroform, they'd been specially cultivated to withstand it.

Little Ria was already waiting for him. He handed her the flowers, simply pressing them into her hands with a slight smile, even though he would have rather given them to her mother. Ria held a finger to her lips and said in a quiet voice that her mother was still asleep. They tiptoed to the kitchen, filled a vase with water and put the daisies in it. Ria had coated her face in a thick layer of matt white powder and her lips were a purplish-red, a mouth to scream with. But she whispered, 'I'll put the flowers in Mother's room. She loves waking to find flowers at her bedside. Do you want to see her?'

They crept into her mother's room. Mrs Mexocos was asleep alone in the big bed. Her red bathing suit was draped over the footboard. Karel furtively touched its knitted fabric as he gazed at her. She lay with her face pressed into the pillow as though she were weeping. But tears weren't flowing. Her breathing was regular and the only thing that flowed was her hair. She lay fully stretched out, flat on her back; the undulations beneath the thin sheet looked to be brimming with health.

Ria placed the vase next to her bed, on top of a packing crate. 'Simply lovely!' she whispered.

'Yes,' said Karel, supposing momentarily that she meant her mother.

Ria rummaged around in a drawer and took out a thin silver chain. Once they'd returned to the kitchen, she put her left foot up on a chair and wound the chain around her silky ankle. Her inner thighs began right above her knees. 'I'm ready, shall we?"

It is Whit Sunday and Master K. Ruis is going for a walk with his betrothed was his momentous thought. But he didn't know what to say, which was why he said, 'Where are we off to?' Ria answered that she'd only just moved into this neighbourhood and didn't know her way around yet. They headed toward the viaduct.

'You should give me your arm,' said Ria. He obeyed and she was soon clutching his hand forcefully. They walked close together as though they'd been acquainted for weeks. His fingers lay lifelessly in her hand. The black-haired girl was much shorter than Karel, she barely reached his shoulder. The little chain around her ankle tinkled with every step.

A soldier was marching back and forth on the viaduct, a rifle over his shoulder. He walked along the rails with slow steps, looking down at the people who passed by beneath him.

'Do you write poetry?' asked Ria.

'No,' said Karel.

'Do you draw?' she asked.

'No,' he said.

'Do you dance? Do you play an instrument?' she asked.

'No, I don't do anything at all,' he replied. 'I'm still at school. I don't do anything special.'

'I don't know why I like you and yet I do,' she marvelled. Then she asked how old he was. 'Seventeen,' he replied.

'I'm only sixteen,' she said, 'but girls always mature much faster than boys. I'm already a woman,' she said. 'I've been one for two years now.'

They'd passed the communal gardens, they walked past a rubbish dump and arrived at a field of cabbages that seemed to go on forever. Ria led him to the grassy verge at the side of the road. She let go of his hand. They sat down and lit cigarettes. Ria lay back in the grass, her eyes closed, hands under her head. Black hair curled from the armholes of her blouse. Karel studied it.

'I'd hate to have to leave this place,' she sighed. 'All that travelling. I've lived in Prague and in Paris. Paris is nice,' she said. 'The French loathe the Germans. But they don't like fighting. They do like wearing smart uniforms and they're quick to anger but they don't like fighting much. Do you think the Germans will hurt us?'

Her face was immobile and pale in the grass, only her eyelashes moved. Love-in-the-mist. 'Of course not,' he said.

'The Germans will never get here. You mustn't believe all those rumours.'

'But what if they do come?' she said. Without waiting for a reply, she sat up and asked, 'Why did you say you wanted to come and live with us?'

'It's nice at your house,' said Karel. 'It's horrible at my house. My parents don't love each other.'

'Would you give me a kiss?' she asked, squeezing her eyes shut and throwing away her cigarette. He gave her a kiss. Their lips rubbed against each other. He lay quietly beside her, their bodies touching. He was happy now. She was his girlfriend. He tentatively stroked her arm.

'If we have to flee,' began Ria, 'you should come with us. Why shouldn't you, if it's horrible for you at home.'

'Yes,' he said, 'why not? Would your mother mind if I came with you?'

'Of course not,' she said. 'She always agrees to whatever I want.'

'That's easy,' he said.

'Kiss me again,' she said. He did so and began to caress her face. The chalky powder stuck to his clammy hand. 'I love you,' he squeaked. After that they lay quietly side by side. He held her hand in a motionless grip as though it were a sheet of paper. Suddenly he asked, 'How do you and your mother know my Uncle Robert?'

The girl raised herself onto her elbows. She sighed loudly. 'Oh,' she said, 'he's an acquaintance, just an acquaintance. He's kind. My mother is very fond of him. He gives me piano lessons. He said he's going to make a brilliant pianist of me.'

Mrs Mexocos had just got up when they returned to the house. She gave her daughter a kiss and then Karel. Her mouth was moist and elastic. 'You need to reapply your lipstick,' she said to Ria. She fluttered around in a pair of Russian pyjamas, an ox-eye daisy behind her right ear. The windows were wide open, Karel went to look outside. Little Ria joined him there, pressing softly and continuously against his side. Behind her back, her mother made swishing dance steps. In the distance he could see the viaduct and the little man with a gun on top of it. Ria was like a cat rubbing its head against him, a warm animal to stroke. There was nothing left of the war but a dark shape on the horizon that would disappear entirely when night fell.

But once it did get dark, the searchlights slid wearily across the sky again and he was back in the sitting room at home. But tomorrow, he thought, tomorrow... Before leaving, the older Ria had said to him, 'Oh Karel, I'm making things difficult for you. Forgive me for still not having written that letter. But there's so little point in writing anything now. Everything is so uncertain. When I write, I want to write something definitive. And I can't yet... Will we see you again tomorrow?'

In bed he thought drowsily: no, no peace, let the Germans come if needs be, then the Rias will have to flee and I will run away with them, why shouldn't I go with them, I won't say anything to my parents, I'll run away, begin a new life in America: California, the U. S. of A., white telephones, Sun-Maid raisins.

9

His mother woke him up at half past ten to say there was a phone call for him. He hurriedly pulled on his trousers and ran downstairs.

'Hello?' he said.

'Karel,' said Mrs Mexocos, 'we're leaving for England this afternoon. Please come immediately.'

'Alright,' he said, then repeating, 'Alright, I'll be there shortly.'

'Who was that?' asked his father.

'No one,' he replied, 'an acquaintance.'

He sat down and scratched his chest under his pyjama top. It was lovely weather again. His brother was sitting on the balcony in his shirtsleeves. It could almost be August. His father said, 'The krauts have reached Langstraat.'

'Which street is that?' he asked, jumping to his feet.

'It's not a street, Langstraat is a region in Brabant,' said his father.

Karel went upstairs to get dressed, skipping up each step like a child. His mother called him back. She was in the kitchen holding his shirt.

'What's this?' she asked, tapping a plum-coloured smudge on its collar.

'Nothing, nothing,' he said recalcitrantly, 'ink, paint, I have no idea.'

'Yes, red ink that smells of perfume,' she replied, sniffing the stain. 'Pull the other leg while you're at it. That's makeup, that's lipstick that is. Who are you keeping company with? Do you think I didn't notice when you came home late, reeking to high heaven of booze? Where have you been the last few days?'

'Nowhere,' said Karel, appearing only capable of uttering outright denials that morning. 'What's it to do with you? Mind your own business, for god's sake. There are more important things to get wound up about at present.'

He looked right through the angry woman. This war was at least good for something. He'd wished for a war, his wish had been granted and the great sea change in his life was about to take place. He shrugged and left the kitchen, whistling to himself.

He got dressed quickly and looked around his room. His books, his school diary, the Rembrandt reproduction above his bed – *Titus Reading* – his crystal set. 'You can have the lot,' he said. 'Adieu.' He shoved a penknife in his pocket, then retrieved a notebook from behind the other books and opened it. On the first page, he'd copied down a line by poet Caesar Gezelle – 'O restless human heart, a tyrant thou art!' On the next page he read, 'It seems to me, as I grow older and life comes rushing, that keeping a diary is necessary. For the first time in my life I have fallen in love. I met her yesterday when ice-skating with Tubs. I accompanied her for two rounds of the rink.'

Karel Ruis grinned smugly. Not even two years ago. A freckled girl who wouldn't stop talking about becoming a nurse. He tore the notebook to shreds. Afterwards he dived into his wardrobe and took out a hockey boot and a stiffly folded copy of *La Vie parisienne*. He tore this up too. He threw the bits of paper down the toilet. As he was flushing it, he said to himself: this is private, they're welcome to the rest, but this is private. Without giving his bedroom a second glance, he went back downstairs.

Everyone else must have already had breakfast, his own was laid out on a napkin. 'What's all this your mother's saying?' his father asked in a serious tone. His father took a seat facing him. A middle-aged man, pulling a face because his wife had ordered him to give his youngest son a lecture about the follies and foibles of youth. 'I heard there was rouge on your undershirt and I want to know how it got there. Where have you been these last couple of days?'

Karel put a chunk of bread into his mouth and chewed. He was completely calm. Won't be long before you get a telegram from London, he thought.

'Have you been to a house of ill repute? Have you been with women?' his father asked.

Listen to that, thought Karel, women plural! He means prostitutes of course, but he doesn't dare say so. Only loose women wear rouge, that's what he thinks. He's a century out of date. Hasn't he noticed that his own daughter wears lipstick? No, he's blind. Mum said shirt, but he's turned it into undershirt, the garment closest to the naked body.

His father gave him a piercing look: a lion tamer who wanted to force his lion to jump through a hoop. 'I'm your father,' he said, 'and I have a right to know.'

His son got to his feet. I can destroy you, he thought. He ran through a few possible lines in his mind, then said in a formal tone, 'Yes, I have been told that you are my father. But sometimes I wonder whether it is true. In any case, I deeply regret the fact.'

At this, he walked out of the door, his head stiff on his neck. He grabbed his raincoat from the coat rack and ran down the flights of stairs. The front door slammed behind him. He straddled his bike with quiet composure. He was convinced his father was standing at the window, watching him go, impotent and sad, as his wife hurled insults at him.

10

Mrs Mexocos opened the door with a mirror in her hand. There were suitcases in the hallway. 'Thank God,' she said, 'I wouldn't have known what to do otherwise! I can't leave without having written to your uncle, can I? He'll be terribly worried. Now where's that letter? Do you think you could take it to him today? Or would that be dangerous? It's very sweet of you to do this. I managed to get two spots on a boat via an acquaintance. It's jam-packed, everyone wants to get away. We set sail at four and it's already half past eleven. There's no doubt now, things have taken a turn for the worse. What have I done with that letter? Ria, have you seen the letter? Oh, here it is.'

Mrs Mexocos looked tired. Her face was only half made up. She was dressed normally now, in stocking and shoes and a skirt suit. 'Do you think it will rain?' she asked, gesturing at a raincoat. 'Oh yes, and here, our house keys. Would you give them to your uncle too?'

Karel nodded and wove his way across the sitting room. Uncle Robert looked down on them haughtily from his black frame. The little soldier was walking back and forth along the viaduct. Karel looked up at the bright blue sky, but no bomb fell, not even rain. Nothing fell. He was alive. His hands grew damp. His bike was downstairs. The door was there. He flicked his penknife open and shut inside his pocket. I'll be off then, he thought. 'I'll be off then,' he said. But Mrs Mexocos had already left the room. Karel couldn't help but laugh. He hit a key on the piano and then another one. *Ping, ping.* Do you play an instrument? No, I'm still at school. I don't do anything special.

'Karel? Is Karel here?' It was Little Ria's voice. He went into the corridor. The sounds of a shower gushed behind a door with a lit-up top window. 'Is that you, Karel? Hello, Karel. Are you leaving already?'

He stood helplessly in front of the door. The door opened a chink. One buttonhole eye and a wet nose and a shiny blue shower cap. Steam billowed into the corridor like gas, and his head began to pound.

'I'm off now, I'm off,' he said.

'But we're leaving for England shortly,' said Ria. 'We have to say goodbye properly. Won't you kiss me goodbye?'

He leaned forward.

'I hate the fact we have to leave,' she said. She was half out of the bathroom now. He stared her right in the face. Her forehead was pink and she had fat red cheeks. She was a girl, a steaming girl pulling him into the shower cabin. She closed the door. Water pattered onto his raincoat. Little Ria clutched him tightly to her body. She looked up at him with a sultry expression. 'I love you, Karel. I will never forget you.'

He put his wet hands on her round wet breasts. Her inner thighs began right above her knees. A very large belly button and a small bulging belly. And the shower kept on gushing. Why didn't she turn it off? My feet are soaking wet inside my shoes, my hair is dripping, but the letter is still dry, safe and dry in my inside pocket. I'll turn up my collar. It's windy and rainy. She's not a scarlet woman, all the lipstick has washed off her.

'Here,' said Ria. She unhooked the chain from her ankle and gave it to him. Her lips latched onto his. What does she see in me? How can I deserve this? What use is it to me? It's over before it's begun. 'Goodbye, sweet Ria.'

'I'll come back soon!'

'Yes,' but now I'm really getting too wet. Why hasn't she asked me whether I will come too? Now she's said she loves me. Why doesn't she beg me to go with them? 'Don't leave me!' She's been a woman for two years already.

Little Ria said, 'I'll stand by the viaduct and wave at you as you go past in the train.'

Karel stood in the corridor, sad and ridiculous. His good trousers had lost their crease. Water dripped down his face, his hair was having a weeping fit. His handkerchief was drenched in a second. He left a trail behind on each of the four flights of stairs. Outside a calm wind was blowing the sand around. He combed his hair and took off his coat. He cycled under the viaduct, past the communal gardens and the rubbish tip to the cabbage field. He dismounted and sat down on the verge. It was the same spot as the previous day with Ria. The half-smoked cigarette she'd thrown away before kissing him lay at his feet. The sun nestled into his clothes. He didn't have any cigarettes on him so he cautiously put Ria's stub in his mouth. The filter was plum-coloured and tasted sweet. He smoked with quick puffs. For the first time in his life, he became aware of smoking actually doing him some good. He realised that it was ridiculous to cry but his throat thickened when he thought: *the very moment I start to love someone she leaves*. And I'm left with nothing. He swore, but swearing didn't help at all. The only thing that helped was the sun. An hour later he was practically dry. He put the silver chain around his neck and buttoned his shirt back up over it.

He cycled straight to the local station, which was completely deserted. An advertising poster on the main concourse – COLOGNE, PEARL OF THE RHINE – had been half ripped from the wall. The torn-off scraps lay on the tiled floor. Karel walked right over them. Only one ticket office was open. The employee was reading an illustrated magazine. 'The next train isn't until six o'clock,' he said. 'And there's supposed to be another tomorrow morning at five, but anything could happen of course.'

The station clock read exactly one o'clock. It was five hours until the next train left. 'If it leaves,' the employee added. And the boat was leaving in three hours. I could go on my bike, he thought. But it's forty kilometres at least. He cycled around the yellow housing blocks indecisively. Would Ria really be standing by the viaduct? What do I care, he thought. But he cycled to the viaduct all the same. She was nowhere to be seen. She was already on her way to the boat, of course. She'll be in England before bedtime, and so what? Why should they have taken me with them? Why would anyone take along a person they met less than three days ago? Everything carries on as usual, even the war. I'll deliver the letter. This whole dreadful business started with that letter. I'll forget the Rias. I'll take the letter to Uncle Robert, who asked me, 'Can I count on you, whatever happens?' In the meantime, an awful lot has happened, but he *can* count on me. I can't go home yet, anyway, they'll be sitting there fretting away. Oh well, they'll get over it. They'll give me a tongue lashing when I arrive home tomorrow but they won't murder me. I don't give a damn about any of it any more.

He cycled around aimlessly, Little Ria on his mind. Crying doesn't help and neither does swearing. Shouting

Fire fire! doesn't help. Shouting dirty words doesn't help. Nothing helps. Because there's no future. The earth continues to turn. The German tanks advance. *Vorwärts* across the Moerdijk bridge in Dordrecht, and backwards and *vorwärts*.

He realised he was starting to feel hungry so he bought a strip of nougat and two sweet buns from a confectionery stall, for which he had to break into Uncle Robert's ten-guilder note. He decided to go to the pictures. He looked at the women and girls he passed as he cycled into town, but without exception none of them compared to Ria and her mother.

The newly dried wool of his jacket began to give off a camphoric smell. He pictured his mother kneeling beside the big green chest in which she kept their summer or winter clothes free of moths. The chest always gave off a thick, unhealthy odour. Everything would stay the same. Tomorrow: the reconciliation scene. And after that? He carried on pedalling determinedly.

All of the cinemas were closed, it turned out. Karel leaned on his bike and studied the stills. *Survival of the Fittest*, the film was called. Pictures of cowboys on horseback or in a saloon, leaning against the counter, and a blond woman in fishnet stockings with remarkably close-set eyes. In front of the UFA picture house, two civilian guards stood on either side of the entrance, which was closed with a barred gate. They stood there, motionless and solemn, as though guarding a royal palace. From time to time, Karel touched the chain beneath his shirt. At least he'd got something out of it.

He bought himself a pack of cigarettes from a vending machine and then an illustrated French magazine, which he sat on a park bench to look through. He smoked one cigarette after another. 'Charles Trenet, the world-famous Singing Fool, visited the Maginot Line to sing for our boys.' It pleased him that he could understand the text. There were also photographs of the hostilities along the Rhine, the war manoeuvres from a week ago. A group of smiling infantrymen clustered around some German landmines; a sign reading *DANGER DE MORT*. A village hall bombed during an air raid, three women and four children had died; the men were out working the fields; what a homecoming! A sad day! The shows at the Casino de Paris had been adapted to the wartime situation; accompanied by a picture of a lady, naked but for a helmet and a gas mask; *Nous continuons* written across her buttocks.

The world continued to turn. Millions of people lived without any idea of Karel Ruis and his misfortunes. They led pleasant lives or died one sorry day. The park still existed. The park was filled with people in summery clothing. They walked past him without so much as a glance. Some were carrying linen bags or metal canisters, hung around their necks like cameras but containing gas masks. The ducks quacked at the children who had come to feed them bread. The swans were just as haughty as the day before. The warm sun kept on shining as though it took pleasure in the earth. There wasn't a single shot fired. Half past two. A blind person passed in a cart, pushed by a girl with springy hair. Three o'clock. The first *blackout paper magnate* has been identified in France. He is fifty-three years old and, until a year ago, was just a provincial manufacturer of wrapping paper. His son is an officer in the air force. Half past three. The Rias are in their cabin. Little Ria is combing her hair with a steel brush and reapplying her lipstick. The boat was ready to steam away. Every square inch is packed with refugees, a ship of émigrés. There's no room for even a mouse, and not for Karel Ruis either. He sits in the park, where he can hear three different clocks striking the hour, sometimes he even imagines he can hear them ticking. The clocks strike four. The boat is leaving. But wasn't there a single place left then? In a lifeboat, in the toilet, in the nook where they kept the coal? Too late, too late! The boat sails out of the harbour. Ria stands on deck waving, but she's waving to nobody. Why didn't I say to her mother, *take me with you in God's name!*? Why didn't I beg her to take me with them? Why didn't I cry, go down on my knees, wring my hands, and kiss her shoes – which she'd designed herself?

Why not? I did nothing, I got under the shower, fully dressed, like an idiot. Saying goodbye like that was so moving: I will never forget you; I'll come back soon…

Yes, but I didn't even say goodbye to her mother, I ran off like a child. It's my own fault. They must have thought I didn't even want to go with them! I've been left behind, backed into a corner behind the New Dutch Waterline.

He began to long for someone to share his pain and confusion with. He began to long for his Uncle Robert. Uncle Robert had a secret too, and he was afraid that his happiness was endangered. Hadn't they both lost their beloved? Weren't they companions in adversity? Karel Ruis jumped to his feet and threw the illustrated magazine into the bushes. Mrs Mexocos's keys jangled in his pocket. He was overcome by a great feeling of joy. I'll go to their house, he thought, I'll go and live in their house. I'll stay there for days. I'll sleep in the big bed, under her covers, between her sheets, in her pyjamas. I'll tinkle on the grand piano. The horsemen will ride through the snowdrifts. I'll look at the patchwork collage of Uncle Robert. The room is white. I drink sherry. I smell eau de Cologne. I take a shower, wash with her soap. I open the windows and let the evening come so that the viaduct sinks away into the darkness. I won't turn on the lights but I'll sit at the window surrounded by her possessions.

Going against the flow of the crowd, he hurriedly wheeled his bike along the footpath to the exit of the park. A voice shouted out, 'Karel! Come here!' He jumped out of his skin and wanted to get on his bike but he couldn't because there were people behind him and people in front of him and he stood there like a trapped hare.

His father walked calmly towards him. He held his hands behind his back, he was carrying a walking stick. He was wearing a green hat but was jacketless. He was walking through the park, strolling pensively in the spring sunshine, looking at the beds of tulips, thinking about the war, a quiet fellow out on Whit Monday, but internally conflicted. And suddenly he saw his lost son and cried, 'Karel, Come here!' He stopped in front of Karel and said, 'Now then, lad.' The lad said nothing. 'Come along!' said his father. 'Let's walk on.' He took his son amicably by the arm and led him back into the park.

They walked along in silence, father and son. When they reached the little café, Karel's father said, 'Come, let's have a sit-down.' They sat down on the terrace. Karel leaned his bike against a tree. He sat facing his father on the quiet café terrace.

'Two beers!' Mr Ruis called. The waiter brought two beers. 'Cheers!' said Mr Ruis. 'Cheers!' said his son. They drank their chilled beers and licked their lips. Beer was more bitter than sherry. 'Cigarette?' asked the father. 'Yes, please,' said his son. They smoked. The clocks struck five. Mr Ruis tapped the paving stones with his walking stick. 'Difficult times, the war,' he commented.

'Yes,' said Karel.

'No one's their usual self,' said his father.

'No,' said Karel.

'We should try to be kinder to each other at times like these,' his father said.

'Yes,' said Karel.

'During these times,' his father began, 'we really need to understand that we belong together.'

'Yes,' said Karel.

They said nothing for a while after this. They drank their beers and they smoked.

Then Mr Ruis said, 'If all the people in the world understood each other better, we wouldn't be in this mess.'

'There have always been wars,' said Karel.

'Yes,' said his father.

'People have never understood each other,' said Karel.

'No, they haven't,' said his father.

They fell into silence again. They drank their beers and smoked cigarettes. Once their glasses were empty, they set off again, the father a little bent-backed, Karel pushing his bike. They walked past a stretch of meadowland in the middle of the park where cows were grazing. The sun glittered through the trees, and the farmer, a regular farmer in blue overalls and clogs, drove up in a cart to milk his cows. They stood and watched as milk splashed into the buckets. They were right in the middle of the city. If it hadn't been wartime, they would have heard the sound of trams, but the trams had stopped running, to save on coal.

'Come on,' said Mr Ruis, 'let's find out what tasty treats Mother has cooked up for us.'

They walked home. The clock struck six as they went in through the front door.

11

IT WAS HALF PAST FIVE before the train chugged into the station. The platform had been packed for more than an hour already. The sun had only just risen. Everything was bathed in grey. Karel had expected to find a man selling sandwiches and coffee somewhere, but he saw nothing of the sort. He paced back and forth and thought: all hell will break loose when they discover my empty bed, but if everything goes smoothly, I'll be back home by lunchtime. He decided not to think about it too much. He wondered where all these people were going. There was a woman next to him with a headscarf, she said she was off to visit her son. Her son was a soldier and she hadn't heard from him for an entire week. She held a bag containing some cake and a new pipe. The woman spoke in excited tones. She showed everyone around her the pipe, 'a genuine Gouda *doorroker* with a ceramic bowl,' and she cracked jokes about the Germans. But nobody listened to her. The train arrived and the crowd began to jostle. It was a steam train that glided regally along the platform.

Suddenly a chorus of voices rose up and echoed in the station's high roof, like a choir in a church. Loud German voices singing an army marching song. A commotion began among the travellers. In one of the goods wagons at the end of the train there was a group of prisoners of war, paratroopers captured behind Dutch lines. Karel went to have a look at them. The Germans were dressed in grey uniforms and some of them were wearing leather jackets. Now they sang a song about kissing blond girls on their red lips: *Blonde Mädel, die küßt man auf den Mund, ja auf den roten rosenroten Mund.* When the guards ordered them to shut up, they stopped obediently, but kept on laughing. They hung out of the open wagon, shouting out to girls who walked past. Nobody seemed to know where the men were being taken.

It was an old-fashioned train with high footboards. Karel couldn't find a seat anywhere and ended up entering a compartment he didn't think was overfull. It was just after six when the train set off. No one felt like talking. The travellers stared ahead sleepily and let their cigarettes smoulder between their fingers. Some of them snoozed with closed grey faces, sitting upright on the uncomfortable benches.

Karel began to warm up. The harbour was tinged red by the sun. The cranes pointed idly up into the air and there wasn't a single ship to be seen. The train moved very slowly, you could easily have kept up with it on foot. Half an hour later they were still passing houses. The train suddenly halted. They were on the viaduct you could see from Mrs Mexocos's window. Soldiers walked along the gravel by the tracks shouting to each other. Their voices were intermittently audible, crackly and impersonal like voices in the cinema. It was quiet otherwise. The locomotive jolted slightly but it was more something you felt than heard. The people in the compartment yawned, cleared their throats and shifted in their seats. Karel elbowed his way to the small window. The city didn't seem to be able to wake up. The yellow housing blocks squatted, bulky and alien, on Mother Earth. He scanned the windows of one of the largest blocks, at the end of the street.

'Anything to see?' a man behind him asked.

'No, nothing,' Karel replied. He watched the smoke from the locomotive slowly drift down the railway embankment and blow along the street with the loose sand. He turned his back on the view.

'I can't think what to do,' the man said listlessly. He was a tall, bony office clerk. 'We're being slowly but surely swallowed up. They've already crossed the Moerdijk bridge and taken all the eastern provinces. It's going wrong, horribly wrong.' He shook his head. 'Swallowed up,' he repeated. No one contradicted him.

'It will be alright,' Karel said, 'as long as the English get here first.'

'Yes, the English,' the man said before falling silent.

Karel felt the fatigue in his knees. Once I've delivered the letter and returned home, he thought, once that's behind me... After that I don't give a damn what happens. I won't have to run off again and I won't have to lie any more. I can just sit indoors and listen to the radio for days... His desire to pour his heart out to his uncle evaporated.

A nagging pain rose up in his loins, making him feel sick. He sat down on the dirty floor, his back resting against the door. When we set off again, it'll swing open, he thought, and I'll tumble backwards into the depths, under the wheels. He let his head drop onto his pulled-up knees.

He was jolted out of his slumber by the train's slow clatter over the rails. He propped himself up and saw that they were passing through deliberately flooded farmland. He asked what time it was. It was around ten. Good heavens, he thought, how long have I been asleep? How long did the train stop for? How long have we been underway again? He couldn't summon the courage to ask anyone, he just sat there and, after some deliberation, lit a cigarette. Ten o'clock – he'd expected to have arrived at Uncle Robert's ages ago. He'd already figured out a plan. He wouldn't visit him at home out of consideration for Aunt Lise. He would call Uncle Robert from the station and suggest they meet in the station restaurant. He could take the same train back, because this was the furthest it could go, given the situation.

They were still moving very slowly but a little faster than before. The polder was flooded on either side of the tracks. The water rippled gently but there were no boats on it, it was too shallow for that. I've done my duty, in any case, he thought. Uncle Robert and Mrs Mexocos won't be able to complain about me. No one will be able to complain about me. Well, maybe my parents. But that makes it mutual, so everything's fair and square.

When the train stopped at a station, he bought coffee in a paper cup and a couple of sandwiches. Someone had got off so that now at least he could sit down. It was eleven o'clock. If the train just kept going he could be there within half an hour. But it was well past one o'clock when he finally got off at the leafy little station in the town where Uncle Robert lived. It felt like he had travelled for hundreds of kilometres. He inhaled the peppery smell of the nearby forest and took in the friendly flowers in the stationmaster's garden. The place was teeming with soldiers, the station's waiting room had been set up as an emergency field hospital. There was a great hustle and bustle, only the prisoners of war did nothing. They hung out of the sliding doors of their wagon and observed the goings on with smiles on their well-nourished faces.

It was an absurd thought that he'd be able to make a phone call here. Nothing was going the way he'd imagined.

Up to now, everything had gone differently. Making plans was pointless, something always got in the way and then he had to start from scratch.

He walked into the village, in the shade of towering beech trees that cast a dappled half-light over the buildings. In the shadow of the church, enormous unmanned cannons pointed up at the foliage. Soldiers lay sleeping in trucks that had been painted green, pocket handkerchiefs over their faces, helmets on their bellies. They also lay criss-cross on the grassy slope of the churchyard. Other soldiers on guard duty, soldiers with bayonets on their rifles, patrolled in a wide arc around them. A field kitchen had been set up on the clipped lawn of a house; soldiers with tea towels around their necks stirred large pans.

Karel experienced for the first time the bittersweet taste of war. Everything he saw would make a perfect shot for a war photographer: scenes behind the frontline. His mind stopped churning, he simply looked. He drank it all in like a draught of lemonade after a long walk, fizzy lemonade.

He entered a bar, intending to call Uncle Robert. It was a small village bar. In the taproom, ten or so silent men were listening to a loudspeaker on the counter. They stood in arbitrary poses in a wide circle around the vibrating green eye, but all of their heads were tilted as though they were about to headbutt something. Karel hovered on the doorstep. He stood there in his crumpled raincoat and listened to the commander-in-chief of the armed forces issue a statement.

'The course the military operations have taken here has prompted Her Majesty the Queen and Her ministers to relocate the seat of government.' The eyes of the listeners roamed around uneasily but they didn't look at each other. The commander-in-chief continued, 'Our troops withdrew last night from the famed New Dutch Waterline. The battle will be hard but it is worth fighting. The independent existence of our people, won centuries ago under William of Orange, is at stake.' The Dutch national anthem followed. The men shifted their weight from one foot to another. When the national anthem was over, they hung around in silence a little longer before starting to talk in a measured hum. They came to the conclusion that the Germans were still not past the defensive waterline in any case.

Karel took a few cautious steps forward and ordered a glass of lemonade. 'Can I make a phone call here?' he asked.

'Not possible,' the publican said, 'the telephone is out of order, due to the bombing.'

'The bombing?' Karel queried.

'Yes,' said the man. 'How come you don't know? Aren't you from around here?' Karel explained that he'd just arrived from the city. 'From the city?' the publican asked, in a tone as though the city was London. 'He's from the city,' he shouted over his shoulder to the men, beckoning them over. The men gathered around Karel suspiciously and stared at him wide-eyed.

'What's it like in the city?' the publican asked.

'Calm,' replied Karel. 'Much calmer than here. There isn't anything to do there to be honest. A couple of bombs fell on Friday and the trams have stopped running and there are blackouts in the evenings. That's all.'

'That's all?' asked the publican. 'No fights with paratroopers?'

'No,' said Karel. 'I don't know anything about that. When I set off this morning, nothing was happening. The train took almost five hours to get here though. There are floods everywhere.'

'So there's no fighting,' the publican concluded. He was about to walk off and rejoin his comrades, disappointed, but Karel asked, 'When was the air raid?'

'Last night,' said the man nonchalantly. 'Twenty dead. The phone lines were knocked down and a whole row of houses.'

'Where?' asked Karel. 'Who died?'

'Well,' began the publican, 'The row was part of the new housing development. Detached houses. To start with, Baron Putsch and his wife and three or four children. Do you know him?'

'Only by name,' said Karel.

'And the building contractor, Smelik. But his wife had just been taken to hospital to give birth. And then… hmm… who else?' he asked a man in a postal uniform.

'That fat man, Mr Ruis,' said the postman. 'Does the young fellow know him?'

'Yes,' said Karel. 'I know him.'

'But his wife was lucky,' said the postman. 'She's at the field hospital in the station.'

'At the field hospital?' said Karel. 'My deepest thanks for this information.' He drained his glass of fizzy lemonade. He counted out thirty-five cents from the four guilders he still had left from Uncle Robert's ten-guilder note. He left the bar.

You see, he thought, nothing ever goes the way I think it will. I can keep on making plans, but making plans is pointless. It's ridiculous to make plans when there's a war on. I might as well have stayed at home.

The letter for Uncle Robert rustled in his inside pocket. 'To Mr. R. P. Ruis, Esquire' was written in a rounded script in sky-blue ink. So Uncle Robert is dead, he thought. He stopped and stared at the unmanned cannons and the idle soldiers. The greasy smell of stewed onions drifted from the garden of the detached house. But Aunt Lise is still alive and she's at the hospital. He ambled down the road back to the station. When I tell my parents that Uncle Robert is dead, they'll forget about concocting any punishments for me, he thought.

The train was puffing out steam at the station. Karel headed to the entrance of the field hospital. KEEP YOUR TICKET TO HAND, he read. There was a soldier in front of the door. There were soldiers in front of every door now.

'I've come to visit Mrs Ruis,' he said.

'We may allow visitors in this evening,' said the soldier.

'But I have to catch that train,' Karel said, gesturing at the puffing locomotive. 'I'm Mrs Ruis's nephew,' he explained. 'Her house was hit last night. Her husband is dead, my uncle...' Anger swelled up in him. 'I have to go in...' he said hoarsely.

'I'll see what I can do,' the soldier said and called out to someone inside. A Red Cross orderly arrived, he was wearing a white apron, his puttees, and black shoes that contrasted sharply.

'He wants to visit one of the air raid victims, a Mrs Ruis,' said the soldier. 'But he has to catch the next train.'

'Come with me,' said the orderly.

They walked through the station restaurant, which was filled with beds containing male patients. Most of them had bandaged heads. The buffet was covered in shiny instruments and balls of cotton wool. Above it hung a portrait of the queen.

In the hall, the nurse tugged at Karel's sleeve. He leaned through a hatch.

'In there,' he said. 'She's in a lot of pain.' Karel looked through the hatch and saw Aunt Lise in an old-fashioned brown bed. She was gently rolling her small brown head from side to side as though she were trying to rock herself to sleep. The nurse clomped across the stone floor and opened the door. 'One minute, no more,' he said.

Karel stood next to the bed. He was struck by how Indonesian his aunt looked. Her head wasn't injured but the covers were pulled up to her chin. Her eyes were open wide with a lot of the white showing. She was staring with her rocking gaze at an advertising poster of an American Indian in a prairie night, who was peering, a hand shading his eyes, at a brightly lit train. THE PACIFIC RAILROAD was written underneath.

'Aunt Lise,' Karel said gently. The skinny lady turned her head momentarily, though without stopping the rocking movement. She didn't seem surprised to see Karel.

'Hello dear, is that you?' she asked in a very clear voice.

'How are you?' Karel asked. He stared at her lips.

'Fine, just fine,' she said. 'But I'm in a lot of pain.' Saliva, released by the shaking, glittered on her chin. 'Poor Robert,' she said. 'If he'd slept on the right and me on the left, he'd be here and I'd be there. Our house burned down again,' she said.

'Yes,' said Karel.

'Now I'll never find out,' his injured aunt said. Her voice began to shake a little. 'I always thought I'd find out one day,' she quivered. 'But now I'll never know.' She began to rock her head harder. Her cheekbones beat holes in the pillow. Her fixed eyes turned with her head.

The nurse arrived holding a syringe. 'Off you go now,' he said.

The boy left without kissing his aunt. He walked through the ticket hall and the restaurant, past all the bandaged heads of the silent soldiers. Outside, the light fell damply through the beech leaves. He walked through the unmanned turnstile and saw the train sliding off slowly between the sandy banks.

12

Karel tapped on the back door of the stationmaster's house. The stationmaster was sitting in the kitchen, eating his dinner. His red cap lay next to his plate. 'Could you tell me what time the next train will leave?' the boy asked.

'There aren't any more trains,' said the man. 'That was the last. It's all military transport from now on.'

'But I have to get back to the city today,' said Karel.

'I'm sorry, but you won't get there by train,' said the stationmaster, before adding, 'And I'm afraid there's nothing I can do about it.'

Karel walked through the flower garden to the street and gazed around indecisively. Perhaps he could get a lift in a car? He walked back into the village, keeping an eye out for cars, but there were only military trucks. He went up to a soldier, who was sitting on a footboard smoking a cigarette.

'Will you be heading in the direction of the city, sir?' Karel asked.

'No,' said the solider, 'but even if I was, we're not allowed to take civilians.'

Karel walked on. I'll have to walk, he thought. Goodness, how long does it take to walk forty kilometres? He bought a bag of white bread rolls and left the village munching on them. He followed the main road, which cut right through the forest. It was hot. He took off his raincoat. All the time he kept looking back to see if there wasn't a car coming. But no, he continued to walk over the pinkish cobblestones entirely alone. He walked through the forest and then there was a deserted village and then a field, just fields and fields. He walked and he looked at his feet and he counted his paces from fencepost to fencepost. He made less and less progress. The occasional cyclist passed by, but never a car, not even a horse and cart. He walked on. He saw the road stretching out endlessly ahead of him, an undeviating road paved with concrete, then tarmac, then gravel, then tarmac, then cobbles. His shoes began to pinch. Now and then he stopped and ate a bread roll. He arrived at the area that had been deliberately flooded, the concrete roadblocks were deserted, a layer of water of about ten centimetres covered the road. He sloshed through it.

Everything is ruined, he thought. They cheated me with their rotten secrecy and lies, he thought. I was impressed by them because they were old or beautiful or acted sincere. They promised me all kinds of things, but nobody kept their word. They died without saying a word or they fled.

He thought about school. The face of his Jewish maths teacher appeared clearly in his mind, his defined jaw, his middle-parting, narrow mouth, with an open grin. He saw a pair of dividers trace circles on the blackboard, a pale hand added lines and numbers and letters... And he walked on. The sun sank in the sky and turned blood-red. The water surrounding him was a red sea. He was walking through an interminable body of water. Soon it will be dark and I'll no longer see the road. I'll fall into a ditch and drown, he thought. Swathes of yellow plants bobbed on the water's surface. Intermittent sections of fence protruded like the helpless carcasses of long-dead animals.

A farm boy cycled up behind him, water spraying high on either side of his wheels. It splashed right over his clogs but he paid it no heed. He stopped once he reached Karel and panted, 'We've capitulated.'

Karel nodded as if he already knew. The boy asked where he was going. 'To the city,' said Karel, and he told him where he'd just come from.

The boy clapped his hands and swore. 'Hop on the back then,' he said to Karel, 'I'm only going a few kilometres but it's better than nothing.'

Karel sat behind the broad blue back, which rhythmically moved up and down. He had to muster all his self-control not to let his head rest against that back. His numb feet flailed in the spray. His only pair of trousers was dripping with mud. Dusk was falling fast and the water turned a drab grey. A wind rose up. The farm boy bent deeper over the handlebars. *We've capitulated*, Karel said to himself over and over, *now we've gone and capitulated*. The Germans will move in and walk our streets. They'll mistreat the Jews. They'll give concerts in the bandstand in the park, they'll play their marching song *Alte Kameraden*. England, London, he thought, all the things I could have done if those letters hadn't needed delivering, if Uncle Robert hadn't come to dinner on Thursday. I could have run away on the first day, jumped on my bike. A rucksack full of food and pedal, pedal, pedal...

They'd left the flooded landscape behind. The fields stretched out before him again. It began to grow dark. When they reached a crossroads, the farm boy panted, 'I have to go left here. You need to go straight on, keep on going straight and you'll get there. Good luck!'

Karel began to walk again. His feet had turned to ice. He decided to stop at the next farm he saw and ask whether he could stay the night. But there weren't any farms at all. Everything was dark and not a single light to be seen. He walked on. He kept thinking the same thing. I'm going home, he thought. My bed's waiting for me at home. My pyjamas are under my pillow. Mum and Dad are sitting at the dinner table, my brother and sister are sitting at the table. There's no such thing as a five-sided table. Perhaps they've already written me off for good.

He didn't come across a soul. There were no planes left in the sky. There were no searchlights either, but in the distance, he saw a red glow. He walked through a village, two rows of houses on either side of a street, and a church. It was deserted. Not a single light anywhere. He didn't hear a sound apart from the barking of dogs. And still he had to knock on someone's door. There was a notice board in front of a tobacconist's. THE NETHERLANDS HAS CAPITULATED he read, and under it, the news that his home city had been bombed and thousands had died.

He left the village. The red glow became visible again and was now much stronger. With each step, the fire seemed to blaze higher. His city was on fire. But he was still at least ten kilometres away. He sat down on the grass verge of a ditch, breathing heavily. War and me, war and me, war and me, he cried out, as though trying to imitate a bird's call. My parents are dead too, I know it for sure. Everyone is dead because of me.

He lay on his back and looked at the tiny stars. The chill of the ground crept into his shoulder blades. Everyone is dead, dead or gone away. What's the point of carrying on walking? I wished for it, he thought, I wished for a war and my wish was granted. My maths teacher will be killed now because he's Jewish. Ria and her mother fled because they're Jewish. They'll never come back, I'll never see them again and that's worse than death. They'll weep that their Robert's gone, because the bombs I wished for killed him. And Aunt Lise will never find out the truth about whatever it was. I said, 'Fall, bomb, fall!', and the bombs fell in their thousands and they buried my parents and my brother and my sister, and Annie and Neel, and the little prince of cheese, in rubble.

He looked up at the stars. Is it possible? he wondered. Is everything my fault? Why didn't they give me a god, a religion, an ideal? They didn't give me anything. Nothing but my own life. I'm seventeen years old. People live all over the world. Where am I to go? Why, he thought, as he felt the cold penetrate his lungs, why did they send me to war this unprepared? Why didn't they tell me what war was like? Surely they knew.

He burst out laughing. They made the war themselves, he thought. They worked for years, slogging away in factories and laboratories to make the very best bombs. Year after year they walked home from their offices and ate their tinned salmon, they wore their pale blue Interlock underwear, their Jaeger, they wore their hair long, they ruined their marriages, they ruined their children, they made music and patchwork pictures, and they were blind and that's why the war happened. Is it so bad to be blind, though? But what will be left for me? Where's my birthright?

He lay on his back, gasping for air. I know I'm the maudlin sort, but my parents are dead and everyone is dead and

Little Ria is walking around London and combing her hair. He fumbled for the chain under his shirt but he couldn't find it. He rummaged around under his clothes but it was no longer there. Of course, he sniggered, why would I ever have been allowed to keep it? Let's imagine I never had it, let's imagine I never had anything. That's easier. I won't have to cry and I can carry on swearing as much as I want.

He heard a car engine in the distance. He saw the vehicle approaching. He wanted to get up, but he saw a glint of something reflected on the green leaves and he knew. He sank down into the ditch as far as he could. He lay deathly still. The vehicle growled toward him. He could vaguely make out German helmets. Maybe they'll shoot me dead and I'll be the last one. There were two soldiers standing on either side of a large gun. The vehicle drove past. Karel sat up to get a better look and a beam of light flashed over him. How could he have known that a motorbike with a sidecar was following the armoured vehicle? He quickly dropped back down but the motorbike screeched to a halt.

'*Werda?*' cried a voice. Karel pressed his face into the grass. His mind was empty. '*Werda, werda?*' shouted the voice. He heard footsteps shuffling closer. Suddenly he was bathed in a bright light. Peering under his arm, he saw two shiny black boots right before his eyes. Kick me now, kick me to death, he thought, but the voice said, '*Was machst du da, was machst du da? Jedermann soll doch jetzt zu Hause sein!* – What are you doing there? Everyone should be in their homes!' The German bent over Karel and shook him by the shoulder. Karel felt the tears gush from his eyes, out of his eyes and out of every pore of his body, like a tidal wave coming over him.

'*Er schluchzt, der Junge,* the boy's crying,' said the German to his companion, who held his torch even closer to be able to observe this spectacle. '*Mein Lieber, was ist denn geschehen?* My dear boy, what has happened to you?' asked the German.

Translator's Afterword

Fall, Bomb, Fall first came to my attention in 2023, when it was republished by Uitgeverij Cossee to mark the centenary of its author's birth. The press drew obvious comparisons to Gerard Reve's 1947 famous novel *The Evenings* (published by Pushkin Press in 2017 in Sam Garrett's translation, and in their classics series in 2023). *The Evenings* is set just after the war, while *Fall, Bomb, Fall* zooms in on the very start. But both novels feature a bored teenaged protagonist, emotionally distanced from his parents, and can loosely be called existentialist. The first edition of Kouwenaar's book in 1950 and a second release in 1984 had not garnered any attention from abroad, but in 2023 foreign publishers finally took note. A German edition soon appeared, to be followed by Spanish, Portuguese and Italian translations. This English edition is likely to open the door to more.

Like most readers in the Netherlands, I primarily knew Kouwenaar, who died in 2014, as a famous poet. I worked for a time for Poetry International Festival in Rotterdam and saw him on stage in 2009, an elderly dude with an impressive walrus moustache. His status was equal to that of the international guests, big names like George Szirtes, Matthew Sweeney, Yang Liang. Kouwenaar's poetry has been much translated over the years, and is available in German, English, French, Farsi, Polish, Romanian and Swedish.

Gerrit Kouwenaar belonged to the Dutch-language *Vijftigers* movement. *Vijftigers* literally means 'from the [19]50s', when this group of Dutch and Belgian experimental writers were at their most active. The movement included Lucebert, Remco Campert and Hugo Claus, and was connected to a parallel movement in art: Cobra, which comprised Corneille, Karel Appel and Constant on the Dutch side, but also some Belgian and Danish painters. The *Vijftigers*' drive for unhindered expression and spontaneity led them to abandon traditional forms such as rhyme and regular verses. They also often omitted punctuation and capital letters in their poems, an attempt to reduce the influence of logical thinking.

However, before he became a famous poet, Kouwenaar had penned three short novels, of which *Fall, Bomb, Fall* (*Val, bom* in Dutch) is the first. It was written when he was just twenty-three and published in a literary magazine, *De Gids*, in 1950. Like many a debut, some of the details in the book are autobiographical. Kouwenaar was born in Amsterdam

TRANSLATOR'S AFTERWORD

and, like the novel's young protagonist, he was seventeen when the German occupation of the Netherlands began. On 10 May 1940, Germany invaded the low countries: the Netherlands, Luxembourg and Belgium. The Battle of the Netherlands lasted for four days, until the Dutch forces surrendered on 14 May. Resistance would continue in the southern province of Zeeland until 17 May, when the entire country capitulated. *Fall, Bomb, Fall* takes place entirely within the space of these crucial few days, when confusion reigned and the Dutch still believed that the British were on their way to save them.

The United Kingdom and France had declared war on Germany in September 1939, after the invasion of Poland, but most of that winter (the period known as the Phoney War) was taken up with posturing and building up troops. The Netherlands, meanwhile, was hoping to remain neutral, as it had in the First World War. This attitude was reflected in its lack of military equipment or a properly trained manpower base. In fact, though they scrambled to improve their army and air force, the Dutch were mainly relying on their defensive waterline to repel the Germans.

During its War of Independence against Spain, the Dutch Republic had realised it could use the country's geography as a defensive measure against enemy troops by flooding low-lying areas. In 1629, construction began of the original 'Hollandic Waterline', which protected the major cities located in the west of the country. The waterline soon demonstrated its value during the Franco-Dutch War.

Later, in the early nineteenth century, the line was moved eastward to include Utrecht, and modernised by adding fortresses. So, after the Germans started attacking Dutch airfields on 10 May, the ground in front of the fortifications, which was below sea level, was deliberately flooded with a few inches of water. It wasn't deep enough for boats but it was deep enough to become boggy and impassable for troops. We see this detail in the novel, first from the train, as Karel notices the flooded polder, and later as he walks back home, sloshing through the water, before being given a backie by a farm boy.

Although Karel Ruis is not identical to the adolescent Kouwenaar, they have quite a few traits in common, as his biographer, Wiel Kusters, notes.* He quotes Kouwenaar as saying, 'On the afternoon of 9th May 1940, I too was bored and stood looking out of my parents' living room window. For me too, my life was invaded by chaos and destruction the next day.' And though the outbreak of war was less of a surprise to him, 'it nevertheless marked a complete rupture. I lived in a different world before 1940 than the one afterwards.'

---

*   Wiel Kusters, *Morgen wordt het voor iedereen maandag. De oorlog van Gerrit Kouwenaar* [It'll Be Monday for Everyone Tomorrow: Gerrit Kouwenaar's War], Uitgeverij Cossee, 2023.

TRANSLATOR'S AFTERWORD

Kusters notes some autobiographical similarities to a number of elements in the book. Uncle Robert, for instance, bears some resemblance to Kouwenaar's uncle Gerrit, with whom he lived for a while. And the first name of the main character, Karel Ruis, bears the alias given to the writer by his cellmates when he spent six months in a prison in Utrecht in 1943. He'd been arrested by the Nazi regime for writing for an illegal underground newspaper, *Parade der Profeten*, which, incidentally, included pieces by W.F. Hermans – some of whose fantastic classic novels are also published in English by Pushkin Press.

The secret notebook that Karel rips up before running away from home to stay with his uncle also exists. Young Gerrit's diary, kept as part of his estate, covers a fledgling crush on a girl he met ice skating in the winter of 1939–40. And the photo Karel remembers as he walks through the park is also preserved in the archive. He is about two years old in it, wearing a hat and holding a letter. He looks at the photographer with a slightly suspicious expression, as if in doubt about the letter, comments Kusters.

The novel's superb dramatic turn is driven by Karel's magical thinking about bombs, followed by the bombs falling. But are these incidents historically accurate? On 11 May 1940, a German bomber that had been hit by anti-aircraft fire over Sloterdijk flew on, but dropped two bombs which hit the red-light district. One landed in the

Blauwburgwal canal; the other hit a row of houses. Forty-four people died and seventy-nine were injured.

A few days later, the entire centre of Rotterdam was destroyed by a massive air raid – reflected in the novel by the red glare over the city as Karel returns home. The setting of *Fall, Bomb, Fall* then seems to be an amalgamation of Amsterdam and Rotterdam.

I'll end with a brief word about the translation challenges posed by this novel. Unlike the style of poetry that Kouwenaar would go on to adopt, the narrative isn't particularly unconventional, and the style is hardly experimental. On the contrary, the writing is pared back and elegant, with a touch of irony. As the mother of a seventeen-year-old myself, I find Kouwenaar's rendering of the adolescent Karel spot on. I often found myself chuckling away as I translated his words, and I found Mrs Mexocos's collage of Uncle Robert downright hilarious: *His lips and ears were made of thick red felt and his cheeks of a natural-coloured shantung silk. His torso was naked and shiny pink too, and below it was a loincloth which was just an ordinary towel, a kitchen hand-towel, blue and grey checked.*

I wanted to convey the book's subtle humour, often dependent on rhythm, and maintain the simplicity of the prose. At the same time, since this is a book from 1950, I needed to aim for a timeless style without any disturbing anachronisms. To create this effect, I avoided any all-too-contemporary slang and Americanisms in my British English.

My translation was produced in January 2024 during a stay at Flanders Literature's Translators' Residence in Antwerp. I worked in tandem with the Spanish translator Gonzalo Fernández Gómez, sharing research, textual interpretations and solutions to the challenges of turning a Dutch text into something accessible to foreign readers. The Spanish edition (*Ojalá cayera una bomba*, published by Gatopardo Ediciones) can therefore be considered a sibling creation.

As well as a writer, journalist and poet, Gerrit Kouwenaar was also a translator. In 1967, he was awarded the Martinus Nijhoff Prize for his translations of plays by Brecht, Goethe and Sartre, among others. I hope my own attempts do his work justice.

MICHELE HUTCHISON,
AMSTERDAM, APRIL 2024

AVAILABLE AND COMING SOON FROM PUSHKIN PRESS

Pushkin Press was founded in 1997, and publishes novels, essays, memoirs, children's books—everything from timeless classics to the urgent and contemporary.

Our books represent exciting, high-quality writing from around the world: we publish some of the twentieth century's most widely acclaimed, brilliant authors such as Stefan Zweig, Yasushi Inoue, Teffi, Antal Szerb, Gerard Reve and Elsa Morante, as well as compelling and award-winning contemporary writers, including Dorthe Nors, Edith Pearlman, Perumal Murugan, Ayelet Gundar-Goshen and Chigozie Obioma.

Pushkin Press publishes the world's best stories, to be read and read again. To discover more, visit www.pushkinpress.com.

THE PASSENGER
ULRICH ALEXANDER BOSCHWITZ

TENDER IS THE FLESH
NINETEEN CLAWS AND A BLACK BIRD
THE UNWORTHY
AGUSTINA BAZTERRICA

SOLENOID
MIRCEA CĂRTĂRESCU

THE WIZARD OF THE KREMLIN
GIULIANO DA EMPOLI

AT NIGHT ALL BLOOD IS BLACK
BEYOND THE DOOR OF NO RETURN
DAVID DIOP

WHEN WE CEASE TO UNDERSTAND THE WORLD
THE MANIAC
BENJAMÍN LABATUT

NO PLACE TO LAY ONE'S HEAD
FRANÇOISE FRENKEL

FORBIDDEN NOTEBOOK
ALBA DE CÉSPEDES

COLLECTED WORKS: A NOVEL
LYDIA SANDGREN

MY MEN
VICTORIA KIELLAND

AS RICH AS THE KING
ABIGAIL ASSOR

LAND OF SNOW AND ASHES
PETRA RAUTIAINEN

LUCKY BREAKS
YEVGENIA BELORUSETS

THE WOLF HUNT
AYELET GUNDAR-GOSHEN

MISS ICELAND
AUDUR AVA ÓLAFSDÓTTIR

MIRROR, SHOULDER, SIGNAL
DORTHE NORS

THE WONDERS
ELENA MEDEL

GROWN UPS
MARIE AUBERT

LEARNING TO TALK TO PLANTS
MARTA ORRIOLS

THE RABBIT BACK LITERATURE SOCIETY
PASI ILMARI JÄÄSKELÄINEN

BINOCULAR VISION
EDITH PEARLMAN

MY BROTHER
KARIN SMIRNOFF

ISLAND
SIRI RANVA HJELM JACOBSEN

ARTURO'S ISLAND
ELSA MORANTE

PYRE
PERUMAL MURUGAN

RED DOG
WILLEM ANKER

AN UNTOUCHED HOUSE
WILLEM FREDERIK HERMANS

WILL
JEROEN OLYSLAEGERS

MY CAT YUGOSLAVIA
PAJTIM STATOVCI

BEAUTY IS A WOUND
EKA KURNIAWAN

BONITA AVENUE
PETER BUWALDA

IN THE BEGINNING WAS THE SEA
TOMÁS GONZÁLEZ